FIRST MOON

A Reverse Harem Tale

Lovin' the Coven Series, book 1

by

JACQUELYN FAYE

FIRST MOON
A Reverse Harem Tale

ISBN: 978-1-945893-05-6

Published by Untold Press LLC
114 NE Estia Lane
Port St Lucie, FL 34983

www.untoldpress.com

PRODUCED IN THE UNITED STATES OF AMERICA

10 9 8 7 6 5 4 3 2 1

Dedication

For my mother, whom I was named after. She had all the talent to be an author but sacrificed everything for her family.

I love you, Mom. And I miss you.

Chapter 1

"Are you sure about this, Dorothea?"

"I am. We've been over this a hundred times, Mother."

"I know, but you were always supposed to stay in Ashville. You were supposed to become high priestess when I answered the Call of our Lady."

"Mother, you are six-hundred years old." I finished stuffing the last of my robes and jeans into my suitcase. My bags were packed. I just needed to stuff my laptop into my backpack and load everything into my car. "You won't get the call for at *least* another four-hundred-years."

"And by then, you will have been forgotten by your coven. How could you expect to become high priestess if that happens?"

"It's not like I'm not going to come visit. I've known these people all my life. But, Mother, this is something I *need* to do. I can feel it."

"The Ninety-Ninth Year Itch is an old wives' tale."

"I'm not so sure." I zipped up my bag and sat on my bed next to it. I'd lived in the homey bedroom since the 1900s. Ninety-Ninth Year Itch or not, it was time for me to move out of my mother's house. Damn near a hundred years was too long. My mother wasn't the easiest person in the realms to live with. If I had to stay even one more year, they might find her stuffed in her cauldron...

"You're being pulled, aren't you?"

I nodded. I couldn't explain it. My birthday had come and gone two days ago. It started as an idea in my head.

Then it became a want. Then it turned into a soul ripping need. I needed to move. Someone or something was pushing me to go north. Straight north and settle there. I couldn't even pinpoint my destination on a map. I'd know it when I saw it. "I can't explain it, Mother. I just *need* to do this."

"I know. The part about the old wives' tale was bullshit. It's how we ended up here, thanks to your grandmother. Lady rest her soul."

"Gramma's not dead. You really need to quit saying that."

"She will be if she keeps critiquing my spells in front of the coven."

"Well, Mayor McGillis won the election. Even with the equine rectum that mysteriously sprouted from his forehead."

"Say it for what it was, dear. A horse's ass."

"And you felt that would stop him from getting elected how?"

"I just wanted to good constituents of this town to know that he is full of shit."

"You're insane."

"I know, baby," she cackled.

I sighed. As much as I bitched about living with her. I would miss her. Sometimes. I looked at her and gave her a sad smile, feeling the waterworks coming. I was going to miss her face, a face that didn't look much older than mine. Her cascading red hair. Her mole right above the dimple on her left cheek...

"You have a piece of chocolate on your face, Mother."

She reached up and wiped the spot off. I was still going to miss her dimple.

"I'm worried about you, you know. Witches, real honest-to-goodness witches have been living in Ashville since...well, forever. People know about us and accept us. The rest of the country...not so much. I don't want to see you burned at the stake, Dorothea."

8

I sighed. Everybody in Ashville called me Dot. My mother absolutely *refused* to call me anything other than by the goddess-given name she had anointed me with. "I'm not going to be burned at the stake, Mother. If anybody tries, I'll just turn them into a plague of frogs."

"Just be careful."

"I'm not going alone."

"That's what I'm afraid of. Josie isn't exactly… safe."

"Two witches are better than one. She'll have my back and I'll have hers. Plus, rent will be half as expensive."

"You have more money than most banks, but that doesn't mean you shouldn't be frugal. I'm proud of you."

She kissed the top of my head.

"It's time." Standing, I walked over to my dresser and opened the lid on my tiny hope chest. I picked it up, set it on the floor next to my bed, and kneeled on the polished wooden floor next to it. The tiny mirror inside the lid reflected my eye as I whispered to it. "*Bhailiú go léir mo rudaí.*"

I stepped back as light flared from the foot-long box, grabbing the suitcase from my bed and stuffing my laptop in my backpack. I slung it over my shoulder and walked toward the door. My mother had already exited the room.

Closing the door, I put my back to it, and waited. The sound of sliding furniture and thunder echoed from behind it. Light flashed through the tiny gap under the door. When the theatrics died down, I opened the door and picked up the chest.

"*Laghdaigh.*" The chest shook in my hand and shrank down to the size of a quarter. I stuck it in my front pocket, looking around the room to make sure it had gotten everything. It did. The only things left were the dresser, my small bed, and the dust bunnies that had been hiding under everything. My mother refused to part with any of them. I reached down and petted one of them. "Thank you, guys."

They scampered off and headed toward my mother's room. They were probably going to get fat living in there. She never cleaned anything.

I grabbed my suitcase and headed downstairs. Mother waited for me by the door. "Are you picking Josie up?"

"Yeah."

"I'll inform Miranda that you are on your way."

"Um. Don't do that."

"Why on earth not?"

"Josie hasn't told her mother that she's moving out yet."

"When was she planning on doing so?"

"When it was safe."

"I see. And did you consider not telling me?"

"Maaaybe…"

"Well, thank you from sparing me the embarrassment. And giving me a chance to say goodbye."

"It's not goodbye, Mother! It's I'll see you soon."

"Very well. Be home for Yule."

"Wouldn't miss it."

My mother rarely hugged me, so it was a bit of a surprise when she wrapped me in her arms and squeezed me tightly. "I'm moderately fond of you, daughter. Be safe."

"I love you, too." I awkwardly hugged her with the arm holding my backpack from sliding off my shoulder.

The front door opened. I pulled back from her embrace. "See? Even house is telling me to get the hell out." The light in the hallway flickered.

"Goodbye, Dorothea."

"Bye, Mother."

I pulled my suitcase through the door and let it *bump bump bump* down the three stone steps. The early November breeze sent a chill through me as I looked over my shoulder at my home. Mother had yet to take down the Samhain decorations. A few days before the start of yule, she'd probably be outside panicking, casting decorations all over it until it looked like a Pinterest page.

10

"*Oscailte,*" I called out to my little Kia Soul. The trunk popped open, and I put my suitcase in and set my backpack on top of it.

"You had better send me a post when you get settled. Let me know where you are!"

"There's these things called cell phones, Mother. You should get one."

"That technology you're so fond of will take *centuries* off your life. How many times have I told you that?"

"Bye!" I got in my car and shut my door. My mother, Madeline, was a bit of a technophobe. It was one of her least endearing qualities. Most witches were. Josie would use them, but she had tech-tarded tendencies. I was obsessive compulsive. I bought *all* the shinies. Human technology fascinated me.

I started the engine and headed toward Josie's house. I texted and drove, shame on me, but being immortal had its perks.

On my way.

KK. Usual Spot.

All Ok?

Nay. IF u see mom, keep driving.

I laughed and touched my phone to the holder. It grabbed it from my hand and pointed the screen toward me. My phone screen faded, and faint blue lines began to glow on the screen. They moved as I passed the streets of Ashville. A wiggling pink dot appeared at the top. That would be my best friend, Josephine. I'd known her since we'd been born on the same day almost a century ago. She was my twin from another witch. Two witches born on All Hallows Eve had caused quite the stir in our sleepy little town.

The pink dot moved closer to the glowing blue dot. I was *that* dot. Magic GPS. Needed no updates, used zero data, and wasn't reliant on human satellites. If I could market it, I'd be a billionaire. My mother would probably kill me for outing witches worldwide, but I still felt half-tempted.

I saw Josie standing beside the road across from her house. She had an anxious look on her face and was nearly bouncing where she stood, glancing nervously at her house. I slowed down, and she tossed her bag in the back and nearly jumped in the front seat.

"Go!"

I gave the car a little gas and we were off.

"Do you see her anywhere?"

I glanced out the window and in the mirrors. "Negative, Pink-rider. The pattern is clear."

"You are so weird."

"Says the expert."

"So where are we heading?"

"North."

"Did you make a playlist?"

"Does my mother smell like mothballs?"

"Put it on! Road. Trip!"

∞ ∞ ∞

The sun breached the horizon and burned my retinas. Not really, but it felt like it. Grabbing my sunglasses out of the center console, I slipped them on. I turned up the music a little to drown out the sounds of Josie's snoring.

The Devil Went Down to Georgia, started and I found myself singing along. Okay, talking really fast along, since there wasn't really any singing. "Country rap," I said and turned it up a little more.

We had crossed the border into Pennsylvania a few hours ago. I felt the pull to go farther west and just followed my gut, ignoring my GPS. The sunlight illuminated the valley nestled *well* below the highway we were traveling. I gave a little gasp. I'd never seen anything quite like it before. It was my first time in the mountains.

"We're getting closer, " I said to myself, since my best friend was in no condition to have a conversation. When she slept, you could set off small explosions by her head and she wouldn't wake up. Literally. I had to bespell her hair back to normal and ended up grounded for a few months, but it had been totally worth it.

Blue flashing lights flickered to life behind me, and a siren started wailing. I sighed, glancing down at my speed. I was only doing five above the speed limit. I slowed down and tried to find a place to pull over, but the road edged right up to the mountain. I kept going for a mile or so until it opened back up. The police officer pulled in behind me.

I shut my car off and rolled down my window.

"Evening Miss. License and registration, please?"

I opened the glove compartment and snagged my registration. Handing both to him, I nervously placed my hands on the wheel and stared out the windshield, Josie's snores filling the vehicle.

"Your friend seems kind of out of it. Late night?"

I looked up at the officer. His blue eyes were framed by light brown lashes, just a shade darker than the gorgeous set of hair on his head. I briefly wondered what it would take to get him to put me in handcuffs...

"Yeah. We've been driving all night."

"Where are you headed?"

"North."

"Canada?"

"Maybe. I'll know when I get there," I said with a small smile.

"Well, get some rest. You were swerving, that's why I pulled you over. You haven't been drinking, have you?"

"No, sir."

"Should I do a field sobriety test?"

"Z-y-x-w-v-u-t-s-r-q-p-o-n-m-l-k-j-i-h-g-f-e-d-c-b-a."

"Whoa."

"Just one of my many talents."

He paused a moment and handed me my license and registration. "Any others I should know about?"

"I could turn you into a toad."

His laugh sent a small shiver down my spine. "Well, we wouldn't want that, ma'am. Hard to pull over pretty ladies for swerving in the mountains when you're a frog."

"Toad."

"That, too. Be careful. There's a hotel a few miles up the road. Pull in there and get some sleep."

"I will. Or I'll wake my lethargic friend up and make her drive."

He tipped his hat and walked back to his car. I almost sighed in disappointment. The officer wasn't your average cop. In fact, I didn't even know hot cops actually existed. We didn't have a decent looking one in Ashville, but the entire police force consisted of the chief and four other officers...

I felt an unfamiliar tugging in my chest. "Don't tell me I'm already homesick," I said to myself in the rearview mirror.

"He was cute."

"You were awake?" I pulled back onto the highway.

"For most of it. I see you stunned him with your reverse alphabet memorization. I told you that would come in handy one day."

"He probably just thinks I'm a smartass."

"He called you pretty..."

"So? Did you want me to offer myself to him in the back of my Kia? In front of my friend?"

"I wouldn't have minded watching..."

"You're a perv."

"Ha. It's been longer for me than you. What was it? 1997?"

"Yeah. About then."

"This is why I agreed to move with you. Living with my parents..."

"Witches on the loose." I held up my fist and Josie didn't leave me hanging.

"So, where the hell are we?"

"Almost to New York."

"City?"

"State."

"That's much less exiting. How long until we get to the city?"

"We're not. We're going way west of there."

"Well turn east. I wanna see the city."

"You knew we were following my itch. I don't have any control of the destination."

"Then turn around. The cop is back there. I'm sure he can quell your itch…"

"Perv."

"We already established that fact."

I caught a quick glance at one of the blue information signs on the side of the road. We were only eight miles from the New York Welcome Center. "Feel like driving?"

"You tired?"

"Apparently. I didn't even realize I was swerving back there."

"You sure you were? Sometimes cops just like to pull over pretty young ladies."

"Uh huh. Sure they do."

"Saw it on a video."

"Maybe in a porn movie. Plumbers aren't that attractive either… Stick to reality, Josie."

"That's no fun."

Josie cranked the speakers and we sang until we pulled off into the rest area. "I gotta pee."

"Me, too."

The place was nearly deserted. Only a couple of semis littered the large parking area reserved for them, and one motor home. In the car area it was just us and a blue pickup. Two guys sat on a picnic table in front of it, smoking cigarettes and leaning back. I parked as close to the entrance as possible.

"Do you want your jacket?"

I shook my head. It was warm enough in the car, but New York in November wasn't exactly pleasant. It wasn't worth the effort to put it on just to run into the rest area.

"Okay," she said and didn't grab hers either. I could hear the *don't let me hear you bitch about how cold it is* in her voice though.

I practically ran. Maybe I should have grabbed my jacket. My long-sleeved T-shirt and jeans did *nothing* to stop the cold wind from stealing the breath from my lungs.

"It's like twenty degrees colder than when we left."

"Well, we have been going *north*. What were you expecting?"

"Palm trees and margaritas."

"That's the other way."

"I know. I was hoping to find a tropical themed bar."

I opened the door, not even holding it for Josie. She could fend for herself. I heard her curse my name as I ran for the bathroom.

"That wasn't very nice. Ahhh. At least it's warm in here."

"It is." I closed the door on the stall and did my business. "I'm going to grab a map," I called out as I washed my hands after I finished.

"Okay."

I left her in the bathroom. She was probably playing on her phone in the stall. The welcome portion of the center was gorgeous. The back wall was mostly glass wall, overlooking the valley. Stylish sofas were placed all over, giving drivers a place to relax and enjoy the scenery. I didn't feel like doing either, so I headed for the information desk.

The maps were lined neatly in wooden holders by the front. Nobody was manning the desk,so I grabbed one and flipped it open, hoping to get maybe an inkling of where we were headed. The highway we were on ultimately passed through Syracuse before heading into Canada.

I could feel them walking toward the door before I heard it open. Their intent oozed ahead of them by at least fifty feet. I sighed and pretended to focus on the map.

"What's a pretty little thing like you doing in a place like this?"

"Reading a map," I replied without looking over my shoulder.

"Where you heading, sugar?"

Great. Now they're both hitting on me.

I chose not to respond. They must have figured it would help their case if they touched me. One of them put his hand on my shoulder, trying to get me to turn around. I folded up the map and set it on the counter in front of me, not wanting to get blood on it.

I turned and rolled my eyes. "Guys. It's been a long night. I'm not interested. In fact, I'm a *lesbian*," I lied.

"That's okay. We won't mind watching you and your pretty friend."

"Okay. I'm not actually gay. I just said that so you would leave me alone. But I'm still not interested."

"We just want to buy you a drink." The one missing a front tooth reached up and caressed my cheek with the back of his hand. I wasn't afraid. Being immortal gave you a certain boost to your confidence levels, even more than tequila. But I didn't want to retch on his shoes as he disgusted me on every level.

"Nice roofie cocktail, I'm sure."

His eyes narrowed. He grew enough balls to reach back his hand and swing at my face.

"*Ná bogadh*," I whispered. His hand froze, inches from my face.

His friend, who had been laughing and cheering, looked at his friend, confusedly. "Aren't you gonna teach her some respect?"

Ten thousand things could have come out of his mouth that would have pissed me off less. Maybe twenty. "Respect?"

"Yeah. We just wanted to buy you a drink. Then you had to get all feminist on us."

Maybe fifty.

"Me not wanting to go off and have a drink with two guys makes me disrespectful?"

"Yes. We're just trying to be nice and you're being bitchy."

My blood began to boil. I decided to return the favor...

"*Bheith ar dóiteáin*," I said and let more than a bit of power flow into the words.

He screamed and backed away, clutching his head. I could see his blood boiling in his veins. Bubbles ran up his arms as he cooked from the inside out. His face began to smoke as his hair singed, filling the room with an acrid odor. The fire alarm went off and the sprinkler system above us kicked on, dousing all of us in water.

"What did you do to him?" His buddy was freaking out, still unable to move. I released the spell.

I expected him to try and help him or even attack me. Instead he ran out of the building. I looked at the half-charred corpse on the ground by my feet. "Nice friend you have there."

Josie came running out of the women's restroom. She took one look at the scene, grabbed my hand and pulled me out the door. My water-soaked clothes became *very* uncomfortable in the wind.

"*Tirim agus te.*" The water evaporated in a puff of mist, my clothes taking on a pulled from the dryer feeling.

"You can't do stuff like that, Dot. We're not in Ashville anymore. People out in the real world don't believe in witches. What do you think they're going to say when they find that body?"

"Spontaneous human combustion?"

"Hmm. Maybe. Anyway, get in the car. Let's go."

I hopped in the passenger seat and buckled up. "If you see a blue pickup, wake me up."

"Why?"

"No reason," I said and tilted the seat back, letting Josie take over.

Chapter 2

I sat up straight in my seat. "Get off the highway!"

"What? Why?" She jerked the wheel and hit the exit ramp at sixty. Stomping on the brakes, she fought for control and slowed without slamming us into the guardrail. She had to have used a tad bit of magic. I should have known better than to be sleeping, missing all the warnings and warmings we were approaching the destination.

"This is it?"

"You sure?"

"Yeah. Where the hell are we?"

"I have no idea. I didn't have a chance to read the sign. I was too busy peeing myself."

I thought she was joking until she said, "*Calidum et siccum.*" It was the same spell I'd used, but Josie used Latin for her canting.

"Ew. Dry the seat, too!"

"It's leather." I could tell by her face she was beyond mortified, so I let it go. We'd been best friends forever. I'd seen worse.

I grabbed my phone to look at the GPS. The actual GPS, not my magic one. I kind of wanted to know where we were. I scrolled the map up to see what we had passed, and Syracuse came into view. "How long was I asleep?"

"A couple of hours."

"Huh. Well, this is the right way." We looped back under the highway and headed west. "We're really close. You're going to see a small town on the right side of whatever the hell road we are on. You're going to comment on how cute it is. That's the one. Get off this road and then head toward the center of town."

"Okaaay. How the hell do you know all that? I mean I understand magic, but this is kind of creepy."

"Trust me. I can see it in my head."

"Always."

"Awww. Thanks, Josie."

We drove. I was almost sad that the itch hadn't kept us in the mountains. It had vanished while I'd been sleeping. The landscape was still dotted with hills, but nothing spectacular. An hour passed before I knew it. We crested a hill and a town came into view.

"Oh, that's cute–" Josie sighed and slowed down.

"You were planning on saying anything in the world but that, weren't you?"

"I was going to say it was ugly. Something wouldn't let me."

I laughed and scooted forward in my seat a little, anxious to see our new home. Josie turned right as soon as she could, and we were off the county road.

"Main Street." I read the street sign as we turned. "How quaint."

"And unoriginal."

"Shush. Don't make fun of our new home."

"Looks smaller than Ashville. We could move to Syracuse and commute..."

"Yeah. Cuz we'd do so well in a city."

"You don't know that."

"I know you would blow up a bus the first time it missed our stop."

"Okay, maybe, but I was looking forward to a little excitement."

"Be careful what you wish for, Josephine."

She shuddered in her seat. "You hungry?" She sounded excited at the prospect of food.

"Hell yeah. Find a diner. You can always judge a town by their diner."

"Cedar Falls Diner. I guess we're in Cedar Falls?"

"That's pretty. Wonder if there's any houses for sale."

"Kinda jumping the gun, aren't you?"

"No. This is the place."

"You're sure?" She didn't sound convinced.

"I'm sure, I'm sure."

"You're the boss."

"Since when?"

She gave me a sidelong glance. "Really? Since forever. Your mother is High Priestess, you're destined to be High Priestess."

"In like four-hundred-years…"

"I'm not talking about home. I'm talking here. It might be a coven of two, but you know I'm yours."

"Damn it, Josie. You're gonna make my mascara run."

"Oh, shut it. You know you magicked that shit on."

"Tramp."

"Ho."

We both started giggling as she pulled my Kia into the parking lot of the diner. We parked, walked to the front door, and stepped back in time forty-years or so.

The motif of the diner seemed to be teal. That was it. Teal and stainless steel. It ranged from the teal and white checkered linoleum tiles, to the teal and white acoustic ceiling tiles. The front of the counter was teal. The register teal. All the condiment holders…you guessed it. Teal.

"Oh, dear Lady," Josie whispered next to me.

"My eyes…"

We giggled and waited for the waitress. She, and her teal outfit, came out from the kitchen carrying two plates of eggs, toast, and cholesterol. It smelled delicious.

"Have a seat wherever, hons," she yelled across the diner.

I gestured to the booth closest to the door. Josie sat facing the diner. I sat facing the pristinely clean glass windows. I was almost giddy. I could people watch while I ate.

Mortals fascinated me on so many different levels. I don't mean like pets. More of a, let's see how much life we can jam into a century, aspect. Some handled it well and were happy. Some were so miserable they did everything they could to make the people around them just as miserable. The former piqued my interest more than the latter. I usually just liked to fuck with them.

Hell hath no fury like a bored witch.

"Coffee?"

I looked up at the waitress who had silently descended on our table. "Please. And a Coke."

"For you?" She turned her attention on Josie and handed us both a couple of menus.

"Tea."

"Kay. Be right back."

"Twenty bucks says her name is Flo."

"Hell no. You probably saw her nametag or something," I said without looking at her, focusing my attention on the more important things. Breakfast.

"Why do you even bother looking at the menu. You know you're going to have a cheese omelet and pancakes."

"I was thinking of trying something different."

"Sure," she replied disbelievingly.

Two minutes later, Flo set our drinks on the table and whipped out her ordering pad. Complete with carbon copies. "What can I get for you, ladies?"

"I'll have a cheese omelet. And chocolate chip pancakes."

"Rebel," Josie muttered from across the table.

"What you having, sweetie?"

"Steak and eggs, medium-raw, over easy, white toast, and hash-browns."

"Herb, diet plate extra moo, and a kid's meal with kid's eggs," she yelled at the large man behind the griddle. I hadn't noticed him until she had said his name. He was dressed in teal. Cedar Falls Diner Camouflage.

"How the hell is all that a diet plate?" I asked incredulously.

"Well they did have a larger one called the belly buster on the menu."

"I kind of want to order it to see what they call it."

"Ask her."

"You ask her."

Our conversation was interrupted by the bell over the door. I looked up from Josie and my mouth almost hit the Formica table-top. He wore blue jeans and had blue eyes. The rest was just icing on the cake.

"Wow. I think I'm going to like it here."

Josie checked out his posterior as he passed our booth. She looked up at me and mouthed, "Holy shit."

We giggled like a couple of school girls. He turned and looked at us over his shoulder and gave us a little wink. I melted. My heart first, but then lower…

I shifted uncomfortably in the seat. Thankfully Flo brought out our food. "Here you go, ladies," she said and sat everything down in front of us. She even managed to carry the jar of syrup and the ketchup. Flo was efficient. "Can I get you anything else?"

"That guys number?"

She looked behind her at blue jeans at the counter. "That's easy. Its 9-1-1."

"Huh?"

"That's the chief of police."

My heart sank. He was probably married and had twelve kids. Women scooped up cops like chocolate ice cream, then divorced them a decade later. It's hard to squeeze twelve kids out in ten years, but if I were married to him, I'd sure as hell try.

"I know what you're thinking, bumpkin, but leave that one alone. He's hurt. Lost his wife two years ago."

"Oh, wow. He's young."

"She was younger."

"Poor guy," Josie chimed in.

"Let me get his order together. I'll be back to check on you in a few."

"Thanks," I said, almost calling her Flo.

I picked at my breakfast, almost too depressed to eat. I'd really chewed on my Converse with that one. Luckily, I hadn't stepped in any dog shit.

"You want to go over there and give him a hug, don't you?"

"Yeah."

"Let it go. You don't need to go breaking hearts in the town we're moving to."

I nodded, knowing she was right. Sighing, I dumped half the bottle of syrup on my pancakes. It hadn't been my intention. The stuff came out quicker than I was expecting.

"Smooth," Josie teased.

"Not *my* fault. The stuff is like water."

She reached over and dipped her finger in it, bringing it to her lips. "Oh, my Lady. It's *real*."

"Real what?"

"Maple syrup. There isn't an ounce of corn syrup in it."

"Huh." I said and took a bite. Heaven spread across my tongue and warmed my very soul. "Woah."

"Yeah. Okay. Its official. We can move here now."

"Yep. It's been twenty years since I've used anything but the fake stuff. I forgot what the real shit tasted like."

"Your mom doesn't buy it?"

"Mom hasn't cooked in twenty years."

"Probably safer that way."

"Yeah." I shuddered.

Out of the corner of my eye, I saw Flo hand blue jeans a plastic bag. He took it and tried to give her some money, but she just kept shaking her head. He sighed and headed toward us, the door actually, but we were sitting by it...

"Have a good day, ladies."

"Thanks, Sherriff," I replied coolly.

"Chief."

"I was close."

"Kinda. You just passing through?" He stopped by the door.

"Thinking of relocating. How's the housing market?"

"Crashed. Buyer's market, though. Mind if I ask why?"

"Seems like a quaint little town. I was thinking of opening a shop or something and settling down."

"The two of you? Together?"

"Just friends," I answered automatically. It wasn't the first time Josie and I had been asked.

He let go of the door and moved closer to our table. He smelled *good*. His aftershave wafted over me. He smelled like pine trees and manliness.

"If I might make a suggestion?"

I nodded.

"Move closer to Syracuse. Cedar Falls is a town most people move *away* from. Like as soon as they possibly can."

"Maybe it just needs some new blood."

"It's up to you. Don't come complaining to me when you get bored," he said with a light chuckle.

"Is there a bowling alley?"

"No."

"Movie theater?"

"Shut down."

"Jeez. Guess we'll just have to figure out something."

"Good luck! Enjoy your stay. I give you six months..." He winked and headed back toward the door.

"We're going to set this town on fire," I whispered to Josie.

27

"They won't know what hit them."

"Can I get you guys anything else?" Flo shuffled up on our conversation.

"We're good for now. Unless you know a good real estate agent?"

"Herb, you have a couple of customers."

"Herb the cook is the real estate agent?"

"And the coroner. Small town."

"How small?"

"Too small," she said and set our check on the table.

Chapter 3

"Hardwood floors, fireplace, three bedrooms, two baths. Garage is in the rear of the house at the end of the drive. The kitchen needs some TLC. I can recommend a good handy man, though."

I looked around the living room. The house might have actually been older than me. It didn't show its age nearly as well. I was afraid to walk across the floor. "That's okay. We're pretty handy."

"You buying together?"

"No. I'm paying."

"You might have a little difficulty getting a mortgage. House is old, in foreclosure, and property values are abysmally low."

I looked up at Herb. He was very soft spoken. I found it almost soothing. "Paying cash."

"You have fifty thousand dollars in the bank?" He seemed a little shocked.

"Yep. I'll take it." The itch seemed happy with my decision.

"It's your loss."

"If you think so little of it, why show it to me?" I was curious.

"Cheapest house in the area, even with the crap market values, but it has the most potential. If you fix it up and the market ever swings the other direction, you might actually make your money back."

"Are you looking out for me, Herb?"

He nodded and blushed.

"Thank you!" I gave him a quick hug. "Let's talk commercial properties now. I'm thinking about opening a bookstore and coffee shop. Have anything in mind?"

He stared at me in shock. "In Cedar Falls?"

"Yep. I hate commuting to work."

"Dorothea…"

"Dot, please. I hate that name."

"Do yourself a favor. Don't waste your money. You dump everything into a business, it's just going to fail in this town. The kids are more interested in smoking weed than reading a book. The married people are obsessed with moving to Syracuse. The older people are obsessed with moving to Florida. A book store coffee shop just won't make it…"

"You still looking out for me, Herb?"

"Yes!"

"Thank you. But, don't worry. Even if it takes twenty years to finally turn a profit, I have enough of a nest egg to survive. I'm doing this because I *want* to."

He sighed, defeatedly. But then he began to think about it. "I might know a place. County property that didn't sell in the last auction… I might be able to get a bid into the council. Let them vote on it. You might even get it cheaper than this place."

"That would be awesome! I'll eat at your diner three meals a day if it's close enough."

"It's actually a couple of buildings down from the diner. Used to be the fire house until it…caught on fire. They built a new one closer to the center of town. It's the newest building in Cedar Falls and it's almost twenty years old."

"How bad was the fire damage?"

"Nothing structural. Some damage to the walls and floors, but nothing that can't be fixed. They built a new firehouse because the old one wouldn't hold a tall enough truck."

"Cool. Can we take a look at it?"

"Sure. Follow me."

We exited the house and I caressed the front door. I whispered I'd be back to make it happy. I could almost hear the house sigh. What most mortals didn't realize is that the more that inanimate objects were bombarded with emotion, the more animated they became. Humans just couldn't hear or see it. The ones that could usually ended up in padded rooms.

Herb got into his baby blue Buick and I got into my Soul. Josie had checked into the one and only motel in town. She was leaving everything up to me since it was my calling and not hers. I pulled away from the house and got behind Herb. We made a few turns and ended up back on Main, heading the way we had come.

We passed the diner and I smiled at the sad oaks lining the road. They grew straight from the wide sidewalks. Most of the buildings butted up to it, not set back like they had been at home. It really was a cute little town. I wished it the best.

Herb pulled into a gap between buildings opening into a smallish black-topped parking lot. The brick building to our right had a large scorch mark on the side.

This must be the fire house. How ironic.

I parked next to the Buick and got out of the car. Herb motioned to the front of the building. It was two stories. Had ample parking. When we turned the corner, half of the front was a double garage door. It had potential. They could be replaced or modified to accommodate sidewalk seating for the coffee shop. If the city ordinances allowed it. I looked around at the other shops. Many were boarded up or empty. I had a feeling the city council might allow sidewalk stripper poles as long as it brought in some business. The town needed a *lot* of work. Luckily, I had plenty of time.

He pulled out a large keyring and unlocked the front door. It would need to be replaced with something a little more business friendly, but once he opened the door, my soul sang. I could feel the blood, sweat, tears, and joy that had been left over the years. The firehouse was lonely. "I'll take it. Sight unseen."

"What?"

"I want this building, Herb. I need this building. I already have ten thousand ideas for the store and I haven't even been inside. If I see any more, I won't be able to sleep tonight."

"You sure?"

I nodded. "Positive."

"Okay. Come by the diner this afternoon. I'll have the house papers ready for you to sign and hopefully I'll have an answer about the firehouse from the county."

"Thanks, Herb," I said and held out my hand. "*Ádh mór*," I said as he shook it. I pushed a bit of power into him. His eyes glazed over for a moment and he shook his head, looking down at my hand.

"What was that?"

"Irish, for good luck."

"It was very pretty. You speak Irish?"

I nodded.

"You're a very interesting young lady, Dot."

"Thanks, Herb. You're pretty interesting yourself. I'll see you this afternoon."

He nodded, still in a little daze. I had no doubt whatsoever that he would secure the deal for the firehouse. Watching him lock the door and walk around the corner to his car, I put my hands in the pockets of my jacket and kicked a rock sitting on the sidewalk, watching as it rolled into the street.

"That's dangerous. A car could have come along and hit that rock."

I looked up at the Chief. "Hey. Sorry, I was lost in thought."

"Was that Herb?" He nodded in the direction of the parking lot.

Herb waved as he drove past us, pulling back out onto the road and heading toward the diner.

"Guess it was."

"Yeah. I just bought a house. And a fire house."

"You bought this dump?" He pointed at the slightly dilapidated building behind me.

"Hey. Be nice. It's going to be beautiful when I'm done with it."

"It was on fire?"

"Herb said there was no structural damage."

"Herb is a real estate agent. They're right up there with lawyers and snake-oil-salesmen."

"My grandfather sold snake oil," I said jokingly.

"So, what are you going to do with it?"

"It's going to be a bookstore and coffee shop."

"Fail," he said and started walking away.

"You're a pessimist."

"No, just a realist," he said after he turned around, still walking backward.

"Where are you going?"

He pointed at the building next to mine. "Police station. At least you won't have to worry about getting robbed. Maybe."

"See you later, Chief."

"Bill."

"Pardon?"

"Call me, Bill."

"Is that your name?"

"No. I just picked it out at random. I always wanted people to call me Bill."

"A pessimist and a smart ass. That's a deadly combination."

"Don't forget realist," he said as he opened the door, entering the building and leaving me standing on the street.

I grabbed my car and headed to the motel. It wasn't even a chain. Farrell's Motel sat just at the edge of main, back toward the highway. It wasn't even a proper motel. Instead of one large building, it was several small cottages linked together with a circular walkway. The motel office and lobby sat in the middle, looking no different from the others. Mr. Farrell himself was the owner, manager, receptionist, maintenance guy, and bell boy. Since ours was the only vehicle in the entire place, even with all the hats he wore, Mr. Farrell wasn't a busy man.

I parked in front of number six. Josie opened the door as I shut off the engine and got out of the car. "You all done?"

"Yep. We have a house and a building."

"Oh, goody."

"Hey. We have a place to live and a means to support ourselves."

"Like you need a means to support you, Ms. Moneybags."

"Not my fault you didn't listen to me on all those investments and savings plans. Seventy-years later, who is laughing now?"

"You. I'm just a free-loading hitchhiker on this adventure of yours…"

"No, you're not. You will be working. You're opening the coffee shop portion of…"

"Of?"

"Give me a minute. I'm trying to think of a clever name for our store."

"Make it witchy!"

"I'm not sure how well that would go over in this town. They might burn us at the stake," I said, half-jokingly.

"Meh. I'd like to see them try." Flames flashed in her eyes. Josie was downright scary when she wanted to be. She had the flame trick mastered. She'd always joked she had an

34

ifrit somewhere in her lineage. I started to doubt her less and less every time she said it.

"Yeah. You hungry?"

"We just ate breakfast two hours ago."

"And it's lunch time."

"Diner?"

"Believe it or not, this town has a McDonalds. Want fries?"

"Only if you get me some nuggets, too."

"You and your nuggets," I said exasperatedly. "Why can't you eat Big-Macs like grown up witches."

Chapter 4

I pulled the handle on the diner, letting Josie go in first. She had decided to tag along with me while I signed everything and then we were going to grab some dinner before heading over and checking out the house. I still hadn't heard back from Herb about the firehouse though, and that was nagging at me.

"Hey, kids," Flo said as we entered. She was delivering dinner to a young couple and their two kids.

"Hi." I waved and slid into our usual booth. If you could call it usual after sitting there once before.

She deposited the last of the food and came over. "What ya want to drink?"

"I'll have a Coke."

"You, hun?"

Josie thought about it for a moment. "Iced tea?"

"Unsweet or from the fountain?"

"What's the difference?"

"About a hundred calories and some raspberry flavoring."

"Unsweet."

She winked and grabbed a couple of menus for us before filling our drink order. I opened mine and noticed Herb waving to me from the kitchen. It wasn't a greeting either, he was waving me to come back.

"I'm being summoned. Order me the turkey dinner," I told Josie and headed toward the kitchen.

Herb swung open the door for me. "Come on back to the office. I have the papers ready."

"How'd it go with the firehouse."

"It's yours. Forty-five-thousand!"

I squealed and threw my arms around him. "Looks like you better get used to seeing me around this place."

"You say that like it's a bad thing. Just don't make Marge jealous."

"Who's Marge?"

"My wife, the waitress."

"Oh. I've been calling her Flo in my head." I laughed. Marge worked, too. I wondered if she'd let me call her Margie.

He led me through the pristine kitchen and into a small office with a desk and a few chairs. I sat down at the mountain of paperwork laid out neatly on the desk. "I'm also the title company, so one stop shopping."

"Jeez, Herb. You're gonna wear yourself too thin."

"Yeah. Cuz eight houses sold in the past ten years keeps me *so* busy."

That came as kind of a shock. It was worse than I thought. For the first time since I'd left on my little adventure, I found myself doubting the itch...

"Where do I sign?"

"Next to all the little yellow strips of tape with the arrow that says sign here."

"Well that's convenient."

"I do my best. I'll be in the kitchen. Holler if you have any questions or finish. The bank is closed for the day. You can drop off a cashier's check for the properties and I'll have everything ready for you tomorrow."

"Sounds good!"

He left me alone in his office which smelled like a combination of Salisbury steak and fried fish. It wasn't unpleasant either. It smelled like diner food, just a little more concentrated. My stomach started growling half-way through the contracts and title pages.

"*Coinnigh ag dul.*"

I let go of the pen and it signed for me as I flipped page after page, trying to keep up. Within moments, I was done. I stacked everything neatly, grabbed the pen from the air, and set it down on top of the stack.

"All done," I told Herb as I exited the office into the kitchen.

"Holy cow, that was fast!"

"Yeah. My hand is numb, and I think I might have left some scorch marks on page thirty."

"As long as it's signed," he said with a wink.

"You need one check or two?"

"Two please. I'll give you the exact amounts with taxes and fees in a minute. You think about it again. Make sure this is what you want to do. Until the checks are in hand..."

"Yeah, yeah. I'm sure. Quit worrying."

"Okay. I will. Welcome to the neighborhood, kiddo."

"Glad to be here!"

I pushed through the door. Josie was talking to a *very* handsome fellow in a fireman's uniform. I sat at the counter instead of heading toward the table. I'd intended on being the ultimate wingman, but she waved me to come over.

"This is my best friend, Dot. Dot, this is Richie."

I shook his hand and slipped into the booth in front of my drink. Thankfully the food hadn't come out yet. I hated cold food. "Hi, Richie."

"Pleasure to meet you, ma'am. I was just asking Josie if she would like to have some drinks this evening. Would you care to join us?"

"I'm beat and have to get up early in the morning, you two have fun!"

Josie shot me a questioning glance. I gave her a sly wink with the eye that Richie couldn't see. "Are you *sure*? Richie says he has a couple of friends who would be joining us..."

Oh. "Well in that case, how *could* I say no?"

"Great. Meet you at O'Malley's at eight?"

"Where is it?" I asked, since I had no clue.

"Corner of Second and Elm. That's two streets north of here and just head west. You can't miss it. There are only two bars in Cedar Falls."

"See you then, Richie," Josie said seductively.

Oh, boy. This is going to be interesting.

He smiled and nodded then headed toward the counter.

"Oh, my Lady. Did you see how hot he is?"

"Scorching. I hope his friends are decent."

"Firemen. I think it's a law they have to be hot. How else would they make all those calendars?"

"Dream on. Remember the ones in Ashville."

"Hey. There were a couple of hot ones."

"Forty years ago."

"Shush. Don't ruin the dream."

Marge brought out our plates. She set Josie's chicken tender platter down in front of her. I rolled my eyes. One day, she was going to start clucking. I was sure of it.

My mouth started watering when she set the turkey platter down in front of me. Sliced turkey sat atop mashed potatoes and slices of white bread. A gallon of gravy had been poured liberally atop all of that and the pile of stuffing next to it. Green beans came in another bowl and a large plastic tub was overflowing with jellied cranberries.

I sliced into it, getting a forkful of everything but the beans and tasted it. It melted on my tongue. I scooped up some cranberries, shoved them in my mouth, and let all the textures and flavors combine into a delightful purview of the afterlife.

"I fucking love turkey."

"You're weird. Chicken's better."

"Shut it, Yolko Ono. Them's fightin' words."

She laughed and chewed on a tender while flipping through her phone. She sighed and set it down, concentrating more on her food.

"Lemme guess, text from your mother?"

She nodded.

"How many?"

"Forty-two so far."

"Did you tell her?"

"Yeah."

"How'd that go?"

"About as well as you'd expect. I'm sure she's casting spells right now trying to find me."

"Shields up?"

"They are."

"Good. I'll strengthen mine in case she decides to start searching for your partner in crime."

"Could you do me a flavor?"

"As long as it isn't chicken," I said and slid another bite into my mouth, stabbing some green beans as I chewed.

"Could you call your mother and have her talk to mine? Your mom was good with the move. Maybe she can calm mine down."

"Mine wasn't good with it. She just accepted that I'm a big witch now and that I would have gone anyway. But yes. I'll have her talk to yours."

"Bless your face."

"You calling me ugly?"

"Ha. You make me feel downright plain. Thanks for that."

"Shut up, Josephine. You're gorgeous."

"This is why I keep you around. You're good for my ego."

"Yeah. Yeah. Hurry up and eat so I can change. I want a shower before we have drinks with the sexy firemen."

"I do, too."

41

Surprisingly enough, we made it early to O'Malley's. I think it might have even broken a personal speed record for the both of us. Which I was good with. If Richie walked in with a couple of overweight, balding flesh bags, I was faking an illness and sneaking out the back door. The bar had one. I checked.

The place was pretty desolate. Sure, it was Thursday night, but I'd been expecting more than four lonely old men sitting at the bar sucking back whiskies. There wasn't even any music playing on the ancient juke box.

"What can I get for you?"

I glanced up at the ancient waitress. "I'll have a vodka on the rocks with an olive."

"For you?" She turned to Josie, very slowly. I blinked when I heard more than one vertebra pop.

"Whiskey sour."

"Be right back. Start a tab?"

"Please," I said and held out my credit card. She waved me off.

"Trusting place."

"Probably easy to remember all fifty people living in this town."

"Yeah, but she doesn't know we live here."

"Fifty people," I repeated. "I'm sure news travels fast. She probably knows our names and address already."

"She's like a hundred and fifty years old. I'd be surprised if she knows *her* name and address."

"Okay. You win that argument. Write it down."

"Woo hoo."

I was saved from her rubbing it in by Richie and his friends walking in through the back door. Luckily, both were hot since they cut off my evacuation route. I hadn't planned on them parking in the rear of the bar. I'd have to file that one away for future date and dashes.

Josie became a beacon of lust for Richie. She saw him and stood up in the booth, waving like a frantic maniac. "Calm down, girl," I whispered to her.

"Is it that obvious?"

"Just don't end up in the parking lot with him. If you want him, take him. At his place. Make sure he isn't married or live with his mother."

"We can't bitch. We just moved out."

"Yeah. Well. Whatever. Shut up."

"Ladies. Good to see you again," Richie said smoothly. "These are my friends, Jimmy and Dennis."

Jimmy was a little taller than Dennis. His blond hair had been pushed back, to keep it from dangling in front of his piercingly blue eyes. They were the first thing I noticed about him. And then his broad shoulders, muscular arms, and everything else. He wasn't just stunning, he was model stunning.

Dennis, on the other hand, was a little more plain, but still a hottie. He just wasn't godlike in his physical perfection. Short cropped brown hair, brown eyes, and a little thicker in the waist. Not a dad bod, but I could see him having one after a few kids.

"Nice to meet you," I said without offering my hand or standing up.

"Wow. You weren't kidding, Richie. They are both absolutely beautiful."

Josie blushed. I smelled a well-rehearsed line. "Thank you," she replied gushingly. I prayed for the ancient one to hurry up with our drinks.

Richie sat down in the corner booth and slid over until he was close to Josie. Jimmy did the same on my side, leaving enough room for Dennis, who oddly stood where he was.

"I'm going to grab some beers. Would you ladies care for anything?"

43

"We've been here for a few minutes. The waitress is getting ours."

"Okay," he said and walked over to the bar. I liked watching him walk.

Jimmy caught me staring at his buddy's ass and smiled. I shrugged and smiled back. "So, you actually moved here on purpose? Is that rumor true? Your car didn't break down or anything?"

"Nope. Was looking to relocate. Just happened to pull into town and said here."

"You might want to reconsider..."

"Everybody keeps telling me that. I'm pretty stubborn, though."

"Is it also true you bought the old fire house?"

"Wow. News does travel fast in this town."

"You have no idea. Telephone, telegraph, and tell-a-Marge. I think she called half the town after you left the diner."

"Which time?"

"Both. I also know you had turkey for dinner."

Unable to stop myself, I laughed. I liked Jimmy. All I got from him was an overwhelming sense of honesty and curiosity. He wasn't out to get in my pants. If he wasn't careful, I might just have to get into his.

Dennis came back to the table, wielding a tray with three beers and our two drinks. "I snagged these from Carol. I figured you'd want them sometime tonight." He pointed at the whiskey sour and then at me. I pointed at Josie. He put it in front of her and set my vodka down in front of me. Then he set all three beers in front of himself.

"That's fucked up," Richie said with a laugh and got up. "You want a beer, Jimmy?"

"Yes, please."

"You got next round."

"Aye, Cap'n."

"Is he a captain?"

44

"Nah. I just like inflating his ego."

"You're a good friend, Jimmy," I said and patted his leg.

"So how long have you two known each other?" He looked from Josie to me."

"Sometimes it feels like a hundred years. We've been best friends since we were born. Even have the same birthday."

"That's kind of creepy," Dennis chimed in.

"Yes, she is," I said with a wink.

"Where are you guys from?"

"Small town in Virginia called Ashville."

"Never heard of it."

"It's not much bigger than Cedar Falls."

"I'm sorry."

"Don't be. Not a big city type of wi–girl." I cursed myself for almost slipping. It didn't go unnoticed by Jimmy either. He lifted an eyebrow next to me.

Richie came back with the beers. We drank and talked and even played some pool. It was a nicer evening than I'd had in a long while. Josie and Richie kept migrating farther and farther from us. Before I knew it, I was leaning over the pool table with Jimmy "helping" me line up a tricky shot. I'd beaten him three out of the last four games we'd played, but he still insisted. I leaned forward farther and pressed my ass against the front of his jeans.

"Careful with your pool cue, Jimmy," I said over my shoulder. Dennis chuckled from his seat against the wall. He'd play winner.

"Sorry, ma'am."

"I wasn't complaining."

It was Jimmy's turn to chuckle. He pressed his hardness into the seam of my jeans. I cursed not wearing leggings. Even so, it was getting difficult to concentrate on my shot. "I see what you're doing now. Trying to cheat and get me to lose."

"I can neither confirm, nor deny your accusations."

45

"Just remember. You started this. Dirty pool."

I hit the cue ball and it snaked around Jimmy's stripe, hit my solid and it *missed*. I should have used magic.

"My turn!"

"It is," I said and moved out of the way for him. The cue had ended up almost exactly where it was when I missed. He bent over, lined up his shot, and I reached down and gave his ass a long caress, just as the tip of his cue hit the ball.

The ball missed his intended target, banked off the wall, and went back down the table, solidly sinking the eight ball.

"Oh, no. Jimmy, you lost!" I tried to sound innocent. I was a horrible actress.

"That's okay. I didn't mind in the least."

I leaned in, putting my mouth next to his ear and whispered, "I bet you didn't."

"Are you going to cheat like that when you play me?" Dennis asked hopefully.

"If you're lucky."

I looked around for Josie. She wasn't anywhere to be found. "Did you see Richie and Josie leave?" I asked Dennis, since he was the one not playing pool.

"They left about five minutes ago."

"I'm sure they did." I chuckled.

"You want to break?" Dennis asked me.

"Guys, I think I'm going to call it a night. I really do have to get up early tomorrow. *But* I would love to do this again sometime. I had a lot of fun."

"Well, we're here most nights we're not on duty. Would you like our numbers?" Jimmy pulled out his phone.

"Sure."

He rattled off his numbers and I really did punch them into my contacts. Surprisingly enough, he didn't ask me for mine. He was leaving the ball in my court. That earned him extra points.

Chapter 5

I turned the large key in the deadbolt and pushed open my motel room door. Hopefully, this would be our last night in the place. It wasn't a hovel or dingy, but it wasn't my own house. I let the door shut behind me and leaned back against it.

All in all, it hadn't been a bad night. Made some new friends. They were hot. Josie was getting laid. I was jealous. Maybe I should have brought Jimmy back to my room. Or Dennis. They were both sweet, polite, and sexy. That was a rare combination. Any one of those traits was rare enough these days.

I pulled off my jacket and my jeans were quick to follow. I didn't bother with the T-shirt, just unhooked the bra and pulled it through the sleeves. I flopped on the bed and flipped on the TV for some background noise. I hadn't been expecting porn.

"Damnit, Josie."

I went to flip the channel, but stopped. They weren't professional porn actors, that much was certain. It was kind of hot. I hated porn porn. This was sexy and real. I let my fingers slide down my stomach and over the front of my panties. I was already well on the way to slippery, just from playing pool with Jimmy. A nice big orgasm might help me fall asleep quicker…

My phone rang.

Of course, it is.

I sighed and got back up, having left it in my jacket pocket. I pulled it out and saw it was Josie. Worried, I answered.

"You okay?"

"Yeah. Kinda. Well, I'm fine, but we were in an accident."

"Richie?"

"He… He um, didn't make it." I could hear the tears in her voice as it cracked. She had just met him, but the connection was almost instant. I knew my Josie, she was a hot mess, but fighting to keep it together.

"Where are you?"

"At the hospital. We didn't even make it to his house, Dot."

"I'm so sorry. I'm on my way. Where is it?"

"Go to Main. If you look toward the diner, you'll see it behind it, a couple of streets back. Three stories. Hard to miss."

"Gimme five."

"Take your time. Waiting for the chief to get here." Then the tears did start. I could hear her sobbing quietly on the other end of the line.

"On my way now."

I hung up and put my clothes back on, the mood completely ruined. Getting back in my Kia, I managed to find the hospital in ten. I pulled as close to the emergency room as possible, but still had to walk a quarter mile to the entrance. Cedar Falls might have a decent population if you counted the half of it hanging out at the hospital…

I almost ran into the glass doors. They weren't electric, I realized at the last possible moment. Pulling one of them open, I entered the heavily sanitized waiting room. Josie was sitting in the corner with Chief Bill. I wasn't even sure if that was his real name, but he was stuck with it now.

Josie had seen better days. Her makeup was nearly pouring down her face as the tears wouldn't stop falling. I nearly ran over and threw my arms around her.

"Are you okay?"

"Been better."

"Give us a minute, please," the Chief said politely.

"I'll be by the vending machines."

"Thanks, Dot."

I nodded and shot Josie a comforting glance. She looked scared. I wanted to do more than give her a glance. I still hadn't even found out what happened.

Pulling out a few dollars, I bought three coffees, two with cream and sugar and one black. I knew Josie liked her coffee light and sweet, but I wasn't sure about Chief. He could pick. I could drink it either way.

A few minutes later, they stood. I grabbed the three cups of coffee and made my way back over, handing Josie hers and holding the other two up to Chief for him to choose one.

"Thanks," he said and grabbed the cream and sugared one. Happiness flowed through me. I could drink it either way, but I preferred it black.

"Are you okay?" First things, first. I needed to check on my friend.

She shrugged and nodded.

"So, what happened?"

"We left the bar and hopped into his truck. We made it halfway to his house when he started feeling sick. Dot, he started sweating. I thought he was going to throw up, but... He burst into flames. As the Lady as my witness, he just turned into a mass of flames. He was screaming and then the truck hit a light pole. Luckily, I got out before the truck went up."

I wrapped my arms around her. She was pretty shaken up. Someone had obviously used magic to kill Richie, the question was why. The myth of spontaneous human combustion was just that...a myth. Chances were it was just a human that pissed off a witch. I just hoped it wasn't Josie that Richie pissed off. Killing humans, no matter what they did to deserve it, wasn't something you did where you lived. I'd only went to the extreme when I was sure I wouldn't be caught. Like the douche at the rest area.

As I held Josie, I looked over at Chief. "Did Richie have a wife or girlfriend?"

"Divorced last year. Please tell me you're not trying to play detective... Leave it to the professionals. I sincerely doubt someone could have launched a Molotov cocktail through an open truck window going forty without your friend noticing or getting hit."

"I didn't say it was a Molotov cocktail. I just asked if he had a wife. Josie and I don't know anybody in this town very well. Just seeing what we were getting into and if we should be worried."

"The answer is no. His ex-wife moved to New York City because of work. Richie stayed and had no desire to leave. They parted amicably and were still friends."

"Thanks," I said, knowing he didn't owe me an explanation or information.

"This is the second one this week." He didn't sound smug, almost...suspicious.

"In town? Two murders?"

"First of all, nobody said this was a murder. We need to let the coroner figure that one out. Secondly, nobody said in town. A report of a similar mysterious death came over the wire. At a rest area on the border..."

"Another burning?" I cursed my luck and tried to sound as innocent as *humanly* possible. "That's strange."

"It is. I'm going to see if I can find the coroner's report from that incident and see what Herb finds out about Richie. Make sure they're unrelated. In *any* way. By the way...where did you two say you're from?"

"Ashville, Virginia."

"Must have been a pretty boring drive."

"Not at all. The mountains were beautiful. First time I'd seen them."

"Have a good day, ladies," he said and walked away drinking his coffee.

"What was all that about?"

"I think he thinks it was me? I don't know. I did do the one at the rest area, but he deserved it. I didn't touch Richie, though." I gave her the *look*.

"It wasn't me!"

"He was a little tipsy. Just making sure you weren't defending yourself."

"No. If anything, he needed to defend against me. I was all over him like white on rice. I was groping him in the truck until he started feeling sick."

"Sorry, Josie. Just asking."

"No worries. Can we get out of here? I need three showers and some sleep."

∞ ∞ ∞

I slipped into the Cedar Falls Diner, almost a hundred-thousand-dollars poorer. I had to wire the money from my bank to the local bank, open an account, and then have cashier's checks printed. The good news was, I now had a local bank and they were *very* happy to be of service. Amazing what a few zeros can do to people's attitudes. I wired over double what I needed. The girl's face was priceless.

"Hey, Dot." Marge set a couple of plates down at one of the tables and walked over to me. "Breakfast or business?"

"Bit a both."

"Grab a seat and I'll tell Herb you're here. Usual?"

"Please. No chocolate chips."

"You got it."

I sat in my usual spot and waited. Marge brought me coffee and a coke before Herb finally slid into the booth with me.

"Morning."

"Hi, Herb. Here you go." I slid the two checks across the table. He checked them over carefully and slid me all the paperwork and keys I could ever want.

"Congratulations!"

"Thanks. When can I move in?"

"Whenever you want. I put the local utility companies' numbers in there on the top. That way you don't have to hunt to get the water, power, cable, etc. turned on."

"You are the man. Thank you."

"My pleasure. If you want to buy anything else in town, let me know. Just not the diner!" He winked and went back to the kitchen. I leafed through everything and called a couple of utilities before my breakfast showed up.

I was still perusing and absentmindedly shoveling food in my mouth when someone sat across from me. I gulped and looked up. Chief was staring at me with a bemused look on his face.

"Hey, Chief."

"Seriously, will you call me Bill?"

"Not until I verify that Bill, is in fact, your actual name."

"Chief William Jonah Bates, at your service."

"Sure."

"Hey, Marge," he called across the diner. "What's my name?"

"Chief."

I giggled.

"My actual name, Marge."

"Dick."

I spit coffee.

"Just kidding, Bill," she added, too little too late.

"See?" He motioned to Marge.

"Doesn't matter. I'm calling you Chief Dick from now on."

He sighed and put his head in his hands. Marge brought him over a mug and poured him some coffee. I noticed he didn't put anything in it before he started sipping. "I thought you liked cream and sugar?"

"Hate it. But I knew you liked yours black. Saw the other morning at breakfast."

"You are definitely a conundrum, William."

"Oh, God. Please don't call me that, Dorothea…"

"Touché. Should I ask how you know my full name?"

"A certain file I was reading last night."

"I have a file?"

"Several. As does your mother. A very recent one I might add. Something about harassing a local politician? Mayor I think it was?"

"Ah. What did that report say she did?"

"Caused some sort of infection on his forehead."

I laughed. "And what did mine say?"

"Mostly mischief and mayhem. That's not what surprised me though…"

"Oh, and what did?"

"How far back the reports went, Dot."

I felt the color drain from my face, which only caused his smile to widen. I hadn't known that Ashville PD had been keeping close tabs on me or my mother. Sure, they knew we were witches, but I didn't think they would have let that kind of information out of the town.

"How far?"

"Thirty years or so. Care to explain how a woman who looks barely twenty has a driver's license that says she's twenty-two and a police record that says she's at least fifty-five? Happy belated birthday."

"Um. I'm sure it's not what you think. I can explain…"

"As soon as you figure out how to lie about it. I'm sure."

"No. It's uh…"

53

He held up his hand and took a sip of coffee. "A man never asks about a woman's age. My mama taught me that. Your hilarious police record and your official driver's license are not why I spent half the morning tracking you down. I figured you'd end up here eventually, so instead of giving up on finding you, I waited."

"What for?"

"Finish your breakfast. We'll talk at the station."

"Am I under arrest?"

"Should you be?"

My mind flashed guiltily to the rest-stop fiasco... "Of course not."

"Uh huh. You have officially piqued my interest Ms. Blackwell. Nothing gets under my skin like a good mystery. I have difficulty sleeping when there are things that don't fit. Things that I can't quite understand. Things that need explaining. You wouldn't want me to lose sleep, would you, Dot?"

"No, Chief Dick."

"That's right. Keep cracking jokes. Finish your breakfast and come with me. Please," he added. I could hear it in his voice. He wouldn't back down, and he wasn't happy.

I lost my appetite...

"Marge, check please."

Chapter 6

"This feels like an episode of Dragnet."

We were sitting in a white room with a steel gray table. The overhead light was shining directly down on me. I was seated in a metal chair that was securely bolted to the floor. Chief Bill had turned his chair around and was straddling it, facing me. The only thing that was missing was a cigarette dangling from his mouth.

"You're pretty funny."

"One of us has to be."

"One of us also is in a lot of trouble."

"So, I'm bad cop?"

"Dot. Enough. Speak."

"Woof."

He slammed his hand down on the table.

"Sheesh. Tough crowd."

He hadn't handcuffed me. Or done anything that would have caused me to burn him to a cinder or turn him into a toad. Yet. I was going to see what exactly his theory was about me and wipe his memory like a chalkboard. That was my saving grace. No matter how incriminated I might ever find myself, I could always wipe the slate clean and start over.

That reminded me. I needed to call Mother and have her make certain police records go away. If she couldn't do it with magic, she always had a backup contingency. She and the Ashville PD often worked together to solve crimes, both mundane and magical. That and she was boinking the chief. He was in his seventies now. I tried not to think about it.

One of his police officers opened the door and brought in two cups of coffee and set them down on the table next to us. I greedily picked mine up and went to take a sip. The Chief reached across the table and stopped me, gently prying it from my grip.

"No talkey, no coffee."

"That's blackmail."

"Yep."

I sighed. It was time to get everything out into the open. I had a house I wanted to move into. "Why don't you tell me what you think is going on."

"You sure you want that?"

"Yes. I'd love to hear your thoughts about me."

"I think you're a witch."

He did it to me again. He said it deadpan and hit the nail right on the head. The man had an uncanny knack for spitting out the truth. I tried not to let any emotions play across my face.

"Well, that's kind of mean."

"Cut the crap, Dot. I *know* you're a witch."

"There's no such thing as witches, Chief."

"Fine. We'll do this the hard way…"

"You gonna beat it out of me?"

He gave me a disgusted look. "Not funny."

"Sorry." I really was. The shadow in his eyes told me it was a sore spot with him and not to be joked about. I filed it away for future reference.

He stood up and walked toward the nondescript filing cabinet in the corner of the room. He took the keys off his belt and unlocked the top drawer. My eyes widened when I saw him pull out a hiltless scian. The last thing I'd been expecting was a dirk. Modern wiccans used them and called them athame. Either way, it was still a ceremonial dagger. He reached back in and pulled out a test tube and a vial of water. I knew in my heart it wasn't plain tap water, either. It was a vial of tears.

Upon a sea of tears, witches' blood doth float.

The son of a bitch is going to test me…

"What's all that?" I pretended ignorance. If he was that well versed in witch lore, he had to be a hunter.

"Dane," he called to the door.

The officer came back into the room. I looked up at him as he strode forward. I opened my mouth to utter a spell when I got hit with one from behind.

"*Rhwymo a thawelwch.*"

I recognized Welsh when I heard it, but not enough to know the spell. I kind of figured it out as ropes grew from the floor and encircled my legs, arms, chest, and mouth. If they had just handcuffed me, I could still have cast spells.

Kudos for using Dane as a distraction. If you think you're going to test me, I'll chew through this fucking rope and cook you like a fucking turkey.

Of course, he couldn't hear a *word* of my mental bravado. But it made me feel a tiny bit better. It at least stopped the tears from coming out when he sat down in front of me with a sinister look on his face as he put everything down on the table.

"You can relax, now. I'm not testing you. This is for me."

He poured a few drops of the tears into the vial. Enough to fill the rounded part. He held the tube in on hand and pricked his finger with the scian. Quickly setting the knife down, he transferred the tube to the other hand and held the finger he'd pricked over the open end. I could almost hear the droplet of blood as it fell into the tube, miraculously missing the sides. It collided with the salt water and didn't mix, like a droplet of oil floating on *top* of the water.

"Do you know what this means?"

"Mmm mm mhmm."

"*Rhyddhau.*"

The ropes snaking around me let loose and slithered back into the ground like some sort of kinky sea serpent.

I worked my jaw, letting the tension out of my jaw. I sighed and stared at Chief from across the table, angrily. "Hey, Dot. I'm a witch. I think you are, too. Look at this spell I can cast." I paused. "You scared the shit out of me."

He had enough common sense to blush. "I knew you were a witch, but you can be a little frustrating. I was making a point."

"Me? Frustrating? Did you just meet you?"

"Point taken. Sorry for scaring you."

"Sorry for being frustrating."

"So, my next question is this. Did you kill, Richie?"

"No. He was on a date with my best friend. Why would I kill him?"

"Because you were jealous? Maybe you didn't like him dating your girl?"

"Excuse me?"

"You and Josie. You're *really* not lovers?"

"No!"

"Oh. Sorry. Just thought that you might..."

"No. Josie tends to swing both ways, but I've never seen the attraction. *But* you already asked me yesterday and I said we weren't"

"I'm sorry."

"No need to apologize. We're just best friends. But, to answer your question, the answer is most definitely a resounding no. I would never get between Josie and her happiness."

"Do you think she might have killed him?"

"She could have, but she didn't."

"How do you know?"

"I asked her."

"You believe her?" He failed to keep the sarcasm out of his voice.

"If she had, he would have had to do something to deserve it. We may not be human, Chief, but we do not take life lightly. It is still a gift from the Lady."

"Is that a fact?"

"It is a fact."

"Want to see some footage from the rest area murder a few days ago?"

"No need. I was there."

"So, you admit to killing him?"

"Did I pull a gun or douse him with gasoline? On record, my answer is no. As your footage will show. His hands were on me when he burst into flame. Must have been spontaneous human combustion. Off the record, witch to witch, yes. I burned him to a cinder. I let my anger get the best of me, but he wouldn't take no for an answer."

"I know. The recording had audio. Don't worry, I'm not pursuing the case. You did, however, completely baffle the state police. They're not even calling it a homicide."

"Well, that's nice."

"The gentleman he was with, however, was booked on an unrelated charge and is now in a psychiatric ward, ranting about how the evil witch made him do it…"

"And I hope he gets the help he needs," I said coolly.

"So, now that we know what is what, and who is who. Why are you here? In Cedar Falls."

"I meant what I said. Looking for a new place to settle. I was pulled here."

Dane gasped behind me. I turned and shot him a questioning look. He looked like he won a couple of grand off a scratch-off. "The Lady provides."

"Provides what? Me?"

The Chief just shrugged. "We are broken."

"I know. I've seen the town."

"I meant the witches in the area. Most have fled, and I can't say I blame them. We… We lost our high priestess. Our coven is shattered. No one received the blessing of the Lady to take her place, either. We wrote to several other covens asking for candidates…"

"I'm taking it that didn't go well."

"No. Two showed up, looked around and left the next day. We've almost forgotten what it means to be witches. We haven't celebrated in…a year-and-a-half? Maybe longer."

Two and two clicked together in my head. "Your wife? She was the high priestess?"

He nodded and didn't say another word.

"Lady, what have you gotten me into?" I asked the air around me.

"I think she led you here to be our high priestess," Dane said respectfully behind me.

"First thing's first. You move over here where I can see you. I don't like people standing behind me. Secondly, let's not get ahead of ourselves. I got the Ninety-Ninth Year Itch. I had to get out of Ashville. That doesn't mean I'm here to be your high priestess. I could have just stuck around Ashville if I wanted that."

"You were in line?"

"Yes. My mother."

"I hate to say it, but you might be here just for that reason."

"Don't you start, too. You've gone two years without a priestess. Don't automatically assume it's gonna be me. Let me get settled. I have a house and a business to bring back from the brink of decay. We'll see." It was as much of a promise as I could make. My mother couldn't force me into a role I didn't want. I'd be damned if a town full of people I just met thought they could do the same thing.

"That's fair enough. Welcome to Cedar Falls from the witch community," Chief said and bowed his head.

"How many are there of you?"

"With the loss of Richie, that brings our number down to eleven."

"Wait. Richie was a witch?"

"Yes. It's the reason he wouldn't leave with his wife. She is a mortal."

"What?"

"Yes. He was the very youngest of us. They were actually in high school together. She was aging, he was not. She had her suspicions, but Richie refused to tell her the truth." He stared off into the distance for a moment. "I'll have to see if I can track her down and let her know. She'd want to be informed."

"More reason to think she didn't do it, then. My question is who is killing witches with magic? And how? His shielding should have kept him safe from a combustion spell. He's the only one?"

"Yes," Chief answered immediately.

Dane coughed.

I looked up at him. He was staring at Chief. "What?"

"Nothing. Yes. As far as we know, Richie is the only one," he repeated adamantly.

"Okay. What's going on? Dane looks like he's about to pop, but is afraid to speak."

"My wife, Rebecca. The circumstances of her death were...suspicious. Even I fell under scrutiny from the Sheriff's Office. We had gotten into a fight, and she left. They found her truck, a burned-out husk, on the outskirts of town."

"Not to sound suspicious myself, but that does sound a *tad* bit like a murder. Before you ask, no I don't think you did it."

"Why?"

"Which part?"

"Both."

"Witches are hard to kill. Fire does the job, but spells can be shielded against. If her truck mysteriously burst into flames, I'm sure she could have magicked her way out of it unless it was instantaneous. Secondly, I don't think you did it because...I don't know. Gut feeling?"

"Well, thank you? And yes. I do know all that. I've thought about it over and over. Did some investigating and found *nothing*. If she was murdered, I felt no magic from the truck or her body." A tear slid down his cheek. "I gave up last year. There was nothing else I could do. And the rest of the coven was tired of answering my questions. It's another reason the coven is no more. I killed it."

"Well, a witch without a coven, isn't. I may not become your high priestess, but I'll help you rebuild what was broken."

"You would?"

"Yes. It's just Josie and I in our little coven now. We have some room to grow." I winked. "Let me get the bookstore open. We can go from there and have place to meet."

"That would be more than...we could ever have hoped for."

Dane nodded enthusiastically.

Chapter 7

The lock clicked, and I pushed the door open. The afternoon sun was filtering through the smudged windows, illuminating the dust motes flying in the swirling air. I could feel the anticipation in the house. It had woken from its long slumber. It was ready to be loved again.

"Welcome home," I whispered to Josie.

She looked tired. I don't think she had slept much the night before. She was still awake when I headed to the bank. Richie's death had hit her harder than she'd been letting on. I reached over and ruffled her hair.

"It's happy," she replied, mentioning the house.

"You can feel it too, huh?"

She nodded, looking around. "It's really cute. Just needs some TLC and a bit of magic."

"No disco balls and shag carpet." I'd seen Josie's taste in home décor. Her bedroom looked like Target threw up. I felt the house shudder in fear.

"Oh, shut up. My room."

"I bought it."

"I'll pay for the utilities."

"Disco balls it is. But only in *your* room. Don't paint the bathroom pink."

"Deal." She reached out with her hand and we shook on it.

I went to the master bedroom. It was completely empty. I wish I could have magicked a complete bedroom set, but it didn't work like that. I could repair almost anything, or even coax it into being something else. I just couldn't call beds and dressers from nothing. The hardwood floors had seen better days. The walls, doors, windows, and ceilings had, too. I sighed. This was going to suck me dry, but it would be totally worth it.

I knelt on the dirty, dusty floor and put my hands against the wood. I pictured what it must have looked like just after the house had been built. Floors shining, pristine paint, clear windows filled my mind's eye. I pushed the magic into the floor.

When I stood, I was standing in a new bedroom. Just without furniture. I hoped Josie was up for a road trip. We needed to find a furniture store in Syracuse and have it delivered as soon as possible. We could pick up a couple of air mattresses for the time being. I really didn't want to spend another night in the motel. The house was mine. It would protect us. Eventually, I could turn it into a magical fortress. It would just take a week or so to get all the spells of protection into place.

I moved to the living room and repeated the procedure. Then the kitchen. The appliances weren't salvageable. I'd buy new and have them haul the old ones away. I could magic floors and walls, but electronics were beyond me. I could have done it if I knew how they worked, but that was a good way to start a house fire…

"Josie, you finish with the bedrooms and your bathroom?"

"As much as possible," she said as she exited the hallway. "Holy crap, you're quick."

"I still need to do the master bath, but we need furniture. Let's head to Syracuse."

"No need. There's a furniture store in town."

"Seriously?"

"Yep. Saw it yesterday."

"Huh. I missed that."

"It's on Main Street. I don't know how you could."

"Everything is on Main. Except the hospital."

"We need to explore one day."

"But today isn't that day. Let's go see what they have, that way we can head to Syracuse if we need to."

Abe's Fine Furniture really was on Main Street. I missed seeing it because it didn't have a sign. The name was painted on the plate glass in faded white paint. I sighed and parked, not expecting to find anything.

Josie looked like she was about to bounce out of her skin. She was *way* too excited about this. I had a bad feeling. Reluctantly, I opened the front door and walked into a 1970s sitcom horror nightmare. Josie looked like she was going to roll around sexually on the horrid couches. I sighed and let her win.

"I'll be by the bedroom furniture. We can get the living room furniture online and have it delivered." I walked away. I just needed a bed. Everything else could wait. Hopefully I could find one I could sleep on without having nightmares.

Surprisingly enough, I found one. A polished oak sleigh bed with matching dresser and nightstands. "Okay then," I said disbelievingly. It was perfect.

"Can I help you, miss?"

I turned around. Assumingly, Abe stood there, hunched over. "Yeah. How much is the bedroom set?"

"Oh, you must be the new girl in town. I heard all about you."

"I'm sure everyone has."

He cackled a dry ancient laugh that made me smile. "True enough, young lady. Welcome to Cedar Falls."

"Thank you, Abe?"

"Yes. That would be me." He focused his attention on the set. "The bed is quite expensive, just by itself. Twelve hundred with the mattress. If you want it without, I can knock five-hundred off. The whole set is two-thousand."

"I'll take it. Do you deliver?"

"Yes. I can have it to you tomorrow."

"I'll throw in another five-hundred if you can get it to me today..." I tried to sound enticing. I *really* didn't want to sleep on an air mattress.

He thought about it for a minute. "Let me call the gentleman who makes my deliveries. I shall leave it up to him. I shall offer him an extra hundred. No need to throw your money around in this town. We help when we can."

I wanted to hug him, but I was afraid I would break him. "Thank you, Abe."

He nodded and waddled slowly to the counter at the back of the store. I decided to walk around and check out the rest of the furniture. Maybe I could help him out and buy a couch or something.

Surprisingly, I did. And a love seat. And a coffee table. And a dining room set. I thought about buying another bedroom set for the spare bedroom but decided to wait. I wasn't sure if I *wanted* a spare bedroom. Maybe a gym. Or an office. A spare bedroom meant that mothers would have a place to stay if they visited... It would be much nicer of me to throw some business at Farrell's Motel.

Abe came back over with a smile on his face. I knew I wouldn't be sleeping uncomfortably tonight. Sure, I didn't have sheets or anything, but it wouldn't be the first time I slept on a bare mattress.

"You're in luck!"

"Great. I found some other things, but they're not a rush. Regular delivery is fine."

"Excellent."

"However, my friend is also shopping for her bedroom. Could you add that to the rush delivery and tell your gentleman there *will* be five-hundred for his troubles. He is doing me a great favor and I insist."

"If you insist. Show me which pieces you want, and I'll ring you up."

"That is the best thing I've heard all day."

By the time I finished paying for everything and Josie chose her stuff, the delivery truck had pulled up to the front of the store. I couldn't have been more surprised. Jimmy and Dennis got out of the cab.

I nearly knocked over a lamp running over. I threw my arms around the both of them. "I'm sorry to hear about Richie."

Their faces darkened, but they nodded. I'm sure they'd been hearing the same words all day. "You guys really don't have to do this today. I'm surprised you agreed."

"If I had known it was for you, I would have done it for free. Richie wouldn't have wanted us to mope around. Giving us something to do actually helps. At least we can think about how heavy the furniture is instead of his loss. How's Josie?" He asked nodding toward her.

"She's a mess. I'm just thankful she wasn't hurt."

"She was lucky. We saw the truck. Bill said someone threw something through the window and doused him. He didn't have a chance."

So that was the official story.

"He told us the same thing. You guys have any idea who might have done it?" I played along.

"Not a clue. Richie was one of the good guys. I've never even seen him get into a fight."

Abe coughed as he walked up. He handed Jimmy my invoice. "Just two bedroom sets tonight." He told them. "There's a few couches and tables for later in the week when you're free."

"Nah. We'll get it done tonight. We don't have another shift until tomorrow night. Let's get these girls moved in."

"Seriously. Don't kill yourselves. Not in a rush on the other things!"

"I'd rather get it all done at once. I hope you don't mind." He winked.

Dennis, on the other hand, didn't look so sure.

"Well, I'll tell you what. You guys load up what you're comfortable moving. The beds are a priority. Everything else is gravy. While you're loading, we'll go get some pizza and beer. How does that sound?"

"Like a little bit of heaven." Jimmy was a smooth talker...

I hugged them both again and let them get to work. Josie gave them a sad wave. "I can't believe they're working. They just lost their best friend."

"Jimmy said it would take their mind off of it." I leaned in to whisper. "I'm sure the money wouldn't hurt either."

Josie nodded in understanding.

"C'mon. Let's go get some pizza and beer for them."

"You're buying. I'm broke now."

"Planned on it."

"You're the best."

"I know."

"No. I mean it. I didn't have the money for this move, but you took me anyway. Thanks for helping me get a life."

"Well, I'll let you in on a little secret."

"What?"

We got into the car and I started it. "The bookstore?"

"Yeah."

"The coffee shop portion is yours. I'll get the equipment for your startup, and the stock. It's yours. You run it. You earn money and you keep it. Don't worry about the utilities and stuff. I already set it up in my name. I was just teasing you earlier. Start saving and stop buying disco balls," I said with a wink.

She leaned across the car and hugged me, kissing me on the cheek and not letting go. It made driving a little difficult, but I managed.

"You really are the best." She managed to choke out the words between sobs. I could feel her tears soaking into my shirt. Somehow, they had dripped in under my jacket.

"Yeah yeah. You're getting me all wet."

She sat up and put her hand over her mouth jokingly. "I didn't think you liked *girls*!"

"Ew. Shut up." My face blushed uncontrollably.

"So, which one then?"

"Which one what?"

"Do you like? Jimmy? Dennis? Chief?"

"What? I just met all of them. Don't get me wrong, they're all hot, but I'm not after any of them. I want to get my shit together. I might have fun with one of them should the opportunity arise, but that's it."

"So, which one?"

"I don't know. Maybe Jimmy. Dennis is sweet, though. Chief, is Chief. He's a pain in the ass and comes with baggage, but he is fucking hot."

"He is. Well, I'm going to stay away from guys for a while. The last one didn't go so well."

I nodded in understanding. I didn't blame her at all. If my almost boyfriend had blown up, I'd stay away, too. "Where's a pizza place?"

"Lemme check my phone."

She punched in the question instead of asking the assistant. I never had luck with them either. While she was busy running a search, I thought about her question again. The three of them played across my thoughts like a sexy slide-show. I was almost surprised when she threw Chief into the mix. I had told her what happened at the station and how they were witches. I told her everything. She seemed to want me to stay away from them for now. Sometimes she surprised me with her protectiveness.

"Antonio's Pizzeria. I'll give you one guess to where it is."

"Main Street?"

"Ha. No. It's a few doors down from the bar."

"Call in an order for two large. One pepperoni, one cheese. And find out where we can buy a case of beer."

By the time we got home, the entire car smelled like a pizza.

"Shit."

"What?"

"Remind me to order kitchen appliances. We have no way to keep the beer cold."

"Seriously?"

"Yes?"

"Did you forget that you're a fucking witch?"

"Do you want to get caught? This isn't Ashville, Josie. Hand a man a beer and he'll drink for a day. Hand a man a cold beer after a few hours, and he'll get suspicious."

"Just put them in the fridge. They don't know it doesn't work."

"Huh. You're not so dumb sometimes."

"I have my moments."

I patted her leg, shut off the car, and we brought everything into the kitchen.

Chapter 8

The doorbell rang. Since I wasn't expecting anyone else, I figured they boys had finally shown up. It took them longer to get everything loaded than I expected, so I knew they had loaded everything.

"Hey, handsome men," I said as I opened the door.

"Thanks, but it's just me." Chief stood on my porch, carrying a twelve-pack of beer.

"Hey, Chief. What brings you to my neck of the woods?"

"I brought you a housewarming gift and came to see if you needed any help."

"You're just in time," I said noticing the moving truck pulling into the driveway.

"For?"

"I bought some furniture. I didn't feel like sleeping on the floor. Mind helping the boys bring it in? There's pizza and beer," I said and took the twelve pack from him, "in it for you."

"Sure. I don't mind."

"You're the most bestest." I motioned for him to come in.

"Wow. You don't waste any time." I heard the admiration in his voice at the state of the house.

"Restoration is easy. You just tell the house to remember what it once was. Especially older houses. They have a lot of personality and power. This one is quite happy at the moment." As I spoke, I could almost feel the house swell with pride.

"I see what you mean." He slid his hand over the countertops.

"Just need new appliances and I'll be all set. Let's go give the boys a hand." I opened the non-working fridge and stuck the beer inside, pulling out four of the ones we had bought.

I handed one to Chief, popped the top on another, and tucked two under my arm for Dennis and Jimmy.

"You're giving your delivery guys beer?"

"Yeah. Friends of mine, actually. Met them last night."

"Jimmy and Dennis?"

"How did you know?"

He just chuckled.

I shrugged and opened the front door. My friends were standing on the porch reaching for the doorbell.

"Hey, somebody order some furniture?"

"That would be me." I chuckled and handed them each a beer.

"Let's get the furniture moved in first."

"I wrangled you up some more help." I stepped out of the way and let Chief make his presence known.

"Bill," they both said in unison, nodding their heads.

"You guys all know each other?"

"It would seem you are some sort of witch magnet," Chief said softly.

"Wait, you two?" I was a firm believer in coincidences. Up to a point. This one had just jogged right on past that and finished the marathon.

They seemed even more shocked than I was. I sighed in frustration. There were spells to locate other witches. There were spells to identify other witches. But, until a witch cast such spells, they could spend their entire lives interacting and not have a single clue. I mentally kicked myself. It should have been the first thing I did upon entering Cedar Falls. I'd been too wrapped up in settling in, I put it on hold.

"You're a witch?" Jimmy sounded hopeful instead of surprised.

"Yeah. Yeah. Josie, too. You said something about furniture?"

"Yes!" I didn't know if he was referring to my answer or the furniture. I didn't care. It would all sort itself out in the end.

He turned around and Dennis followed him. I sighed and leaned against the door jamb. Chief put his hand on my shoulder and leaned in a little closer. "You felt their excitement, didn't you?"

"Yeah. I'm going to be brutally honest, though. The itch was an excuse to get the hell out of dodge. I really didn't want to be high priestess. The odds of me assuming the role here are..."

"Deep breaths. Nobody will force you to do anything you don't want to do. Now it's my turn to be brutally honest, though. You've just given us all a little more hope." He squeezed the shoulder he'd been holding and slipped through the door.

I stared after him. I'd been in town only a few days and had accidentally bumped into five members of the former coven. All of them were men. That in itself was highly unusual and fell out of my belief in coincidences spectrum. I'd ask Chief or the boys about it later. After I had a houseful of furniture.

With five of us, and a bit of magic, we made short work of getting everything inside and set up. The house basics were done. After replacing appliances, stocking everything, and a little bit of décor, it would be a home. My home. I sighed and smiled in satisfaction as I busted out the beer and pizzas.

We sat around on the new couches and ate. By the time I finished swallowing the first bite, I'd already become a fan of Antonio's Pizza. It wasn't even hot and it was delicious.

"*Bheith te,*" I whispered to my pizza. The cheese softened and a whisp of steam erupted from the slice. The crust even became a little less rigid and I took a bite, groaning in pizza ecstasy.

Opening my eyes, all four of them were staring at me and trying not to laugh. "Shut up. It's better warm."

The four of them used their own magic to heat dinner back up. That was probably the single greatest gift from being a witch. No need for microwaves. It saved a lot of counter space.

"Are there any actual women in your former coven, or just hunky dudes."

"Out of the eleven remaining, you know us three," Chief began and paused to take a swig of beer, "plus Dane. There are two more single men, one single woman, and two married witch couples."

"That's a heavily male coven. I'm kind of shocked." I wasn't kidding. Usually the women outnumbered men two-to-one. Male witches were just rarer. My father was a witch, but I'd never met him. Mom met him while visiting Roanoke one weekend, I was the result. Josie's dad was actually human and passed away a *long* time ago. It worked the other way as well. Male witches had offspring with human women. When they came into their power, they would often spirit the child away and raise them or meet with them in secret, explaining their power and what to expect. Having a human parent was more common than one would think. It didn't affect the offspring's magic potential, either.

"Yeah. It's always been like that here, too. My mother told me some of the history of the Coven of the Gold Moon. Way back, they were a protectorate coven for hire. Specializing in combat magicka and fighting."

"That's a new one on me. Interesting," I said and thought of the possibilities.

"That was long ago," he repeated. "We are most definitely not what we once were."

"None of us are," I assured him. "Even for witches, the lure of modern-day conveniences and safety has greatly impacted our need for magic. I am only ninety-nine years old, and even I can see the difference."

Jimmy nodded, understanding my point. Chief seemed a little skeptical. I didn't elaborate any further.

"I do have one question, though. How do you hide what you are from the humans? I mean they *have* to notice when none of you age."

"We stay as long as we can and then move. We're the youngest of the generations. Sometimes they move back, but not in my lifetime."

"That sucks." I gave Chief a sad smile.

"How do you get away with it in Ashville?"

"The town was created by my grandmother. We don't hide what we are from the humans and they know to keep our secret. It's a symbiotic relationship that has worked for hundreds of years."

Chief nodded, but still looked a little skeptical, hurrying to change the subject. "Would you care to meet the rest of our coven?"

I looked at Chief. "Sure. I'll be neighborly. I want to work on the bookstore this weekend, and I still have a ton of stuff to order for the house. Maybe next weekend?"

"Would you care to have some help with the store? You have to be pretty tired after the amount of power you dumped into the house."

I opened my mouth to protest, but the nagging in my gut kept me silent. "Sure," I found myself replying.

"Then, it's settled. What time were you planning on going?"

"Ten in the morning? That too early?"

"Works for us," Dennis replied for them. "We start our shift at 4, so we can help for a bit."

"You two don't need to. You've already helped enough tonight."

"We don't mind," Jimmy added.

I sighed. The people of Cedar Falls were a little *too* helpful...

"Well, I'm going to call it a night. You ready, Jim?"

Jimmy nodded at Dennis and stood up, stretching his six-foot frame. I admired his stomach as his shirt rode up a bit. Josie kicked my foot with hers from the seat next to me. I blushed for getting caught staring.

I stood up to walk them to the door. "Thanks, guys. I can't even begin to tell you how much I appreciate the help."

"It's what friends do," Dennis said.

I reached up and hugged him solidly. He felt good and smelled better, even after moving a truck full of furniture.

"Hey. My turn."

I laughed and let go of Dennis and stepped up to the arduous task of hugging Jimmy. The first thing I noticed, he and Dennis used the same cologne or after shave. They smelled almost identical. Jimmy seemed to be a little spicier to match his personality. "You smell good. Both of you."

He chuckled and pulled back. I didn't want to let go, but I did. "We'll see you tomorrow, then we're on for twenty-four hours. Come drinking with us Sunday?"

"Is the bar open?"

He laughed. "Since it's about the only damn thing to do in this town, yes. Yes, it is."

"We need to change that."

He let go and stepped back. "Change what?"

"This town. Just musing. Yes. I'll see you guys Sunday."

"Bring Josie along. I'm sure she could use the distraction."

I nodded. He was righter than he knew. "Night, guys. Be safe. Keep your shields up."

"What do you mean?" Dennis asked confusedly.

"Shields. Protection from magic?"

"Yes. I know what they are, why are you saying to keep them up?"

"Well, first of all, you should keep them on you at all times. That's Basic Witchcraft 101. Secondly, if someone is out there casting spells at witches, it would give you time to fight back or get away."

"You think it was a spell that killed Richie?" Jimmy said it, but it didn't come out as a question. More of a confirmation of a suspicion.

"Chief," I called over to the couch, interrupting his conversation with Josie.

"What?"

"Did you not warn the coven that magic might have been involved in Richie's death?"

His face darkened, and he shook his head. "No. I didn't want to concern anyone until I knew for certain. I checked the body and truck myself. There were no residual magicks. I didn't want to cause a panic."

"There's a difference between causing a panic and telling people to be careful. You should warn the rest. At least until we figure out what is going on."

"We? Does that mean you're joining us?"

I sighed. The vague notion that I had fallen into a carefully laid trap flittered across my brain. I doubted it, but that's what it felt like. Even if I joined, it didn't mean I'd be their high priestess.

"Yes. I'll join your coven. Josie?"

She nodded and gave me a little smile.

"Yes, to both of us. Now put up your damn shields and be careful out there. If you run into anything weird, call me."

"We don't have your number," all three said in unison.

I squeezed the bridge of my nose, warding off the tension headache I felt coming. "You two I'll text. Go on. Go get some sleep."

They closed their eyes for a moment and I could feel the magic swirling around them before it faded into nothingness. At least they would be protected. I had a hard time believing they, and the rest of the coven, had been walking around without their shields all this time. I wasn't kidding when I'd said it was basic witchcraft. Shields, shields, shields had been beaten into Josie and I since the magic first came to us. It didn't only protect you, it protected everyone around you from inadvertent intent. If Chief's wife hadn't been high priestess for any length of time, her predecessor was to blame. If it was Chief's wife... Well, I'd let the blame die.

"I should be heading out, too." Chief stood up and pulled his cell out of its holster on his hip. "Here's my number," he said, holding his phone up.

I pulled mine out of my jacket hanging by the door and punched in his contact. I sent him a quick text and did the same for the other two. "Pass it along to the rest if you run into them. We'll have a quick meeting tomorrow and I'll pass it around with a warning to be safe. If you don't mind, Chief..."

"Not at all. We've always done as we were told by our high priestesses. When the coven settled in this area, we slowly lost contact with the rest of the covens who used to rely on us... Then there was nothing to worry about. We became way too complacent. My wife was something of a free spirit and never preached, just like her mother."

That answers my question.

"Not being mercenaries and not being safe are two different things."

He nodded and didn't say anything else. I'd struck a nerve.

"We'll discuss it with the rest tomorrow."

"Okay. Thanks, Dot."

"You're welcome, Chief."

"Will you *please* call me Bill?"

"Maybe someday. At least I left the dick off your official title." I winked to let him know I was kidding.

"What the hell have I gotten myself into?"

"You've seen the report. Me and the police go *way* back. Having a witch be the chief of police is gonna be so much fun!"

He groaned and headed to the door.

"You didn't want a hug?"

He turned around and shook his head. "Maybe next time. Or if you start calling me by my name…"

"Night, Chief."

"Night, Dot."

Chapter 9

Herb had made turning the ancient lock look easy. I struggled for a few minutes before magicking the shit out of it. By the time the spell did its work, the brass lock gleamed in the morning sunlight shining between the buildings. It *clicked* open with no resistance whatsoever.

I entered the soon-to-be bookshop with a smile on my face and my laptop under my arm. I'd called the utility departments that morning before heading over. Flipping on the light switch, I could hear the lights turning on with a soft *tick*. Wanting to check the water status, I slipped into the bathroom and turned on the faucet. Rust colored water dribbled out. One out of two utilities wasn't bad. I gave a silent prayer they would have the water turned on sometime today.

I decided to explore the rest of my newly acquired kingdom.

The kitchen actually had nice gas appliances of industrial stainless steel. They might be salvageable and of use in the coffee shop. Maybe Josie could turn it into a café and coffee shop. Sandwiches and such. I'd suggest it when she got there. I'd dropped her off a few doors down to pick up donuts and coffee for the hopefully small army of witches on their way.

The bunk area would make a good storage room. The battalion chief's office would make a nice office. The garage could be the actual book store... I couldn't believe how perfect the place was. The roof was tall enough to add a second floor, maybe with an open center looking down on the first. I made a mental note to ask the general contractor I'd be hiring if it were feasible and how much the cost would be...

I set my laptop up in the kitchen at the counter overlooking the living area. I could practically see the bistro chairs and tables sitting in the cute café. We could even put a storefront in the one wall overlooking the sidewalk like I'd originally planned. I nearly bounced with excitement.

I decided to wait on looking for the General Contractor until we magicked what we could into its former glory. I wouldn't make any other changes until the contractor came in and did his work.

Leaving the computer to boot, I headed for the garage. It wasn't as large as I would have liked, but then again if it were, I wouldn't have a firehouse in my possession. It was one of the reasons the county decided to rebuild instead of repair. It had been built to house smaller firetrucks, not the large monsters prevalent today. A second floor would be necessary to house the stock I'd had planned in my mind's eye. I briefly wondered if there were other nearby areas I could turn into bookstore as well.

Wonder if the police station is for sale...

Wonder if the police chief comes with the purchase...

I giggled at the thought racing through my perverted brain.

As if by magic, the chief came strolling through the open front door. "Mornin', Dot."

"Morning, Chief."

"Anybody show up yet?"

"Negative. Josie will be here in a minute with breakfast, but you're the first."

"Well, it's my day off. So, put me to work."

Dirty thoughts...

"Oh, I will," I purred. "But let's wait 'til everyone gets here. I'd rather you be around to make introductions and then we can have that small meeting and tear into the donuts. You like donuts, don't you?"

"Was that a cop joke?"

"It *was*! Glad you caught that. I hate explaining my jokes."

"You're a strange girl. I should arrest you for...*something.*"

"Cuff me whenever you want. Warning you, I might like it though."

"I'm sure you would." He laughed and looked around the garage. "This place is going to need a lot of work. And a lot of money."

"Yeah. I'm not expecting to be open next week. I'm realistic but hopeful. I'll be calling a general contractor to do what we can't. And build some bookcases."

"You're not going to go with premade ones?"

"No. I want everything to match and fit perfectly. My mother had a personal library. Custom made bookshelves aren't that much more expensive than boring metal ones and look a whole lot nicer."

"Your mother the high priestess?"

I nodded. "That's the one."

"What coven?"

"The Coven of the Dark Spring."

"Dark Spring?"

"Yep," I said quietly, having made the name up for one specific reason.

"That doesn't sound right."

"Really?" *Damn him and his unnatural ability to see through lies.*

"Yeah. Dark Spring? Like as in the season or water? Hmmm. Dark spring almost sounds like black well..."

Shit. "Fine. You're right."

"Huh?"

"Yes. The coven is Black Well."

"Isn't that your last name?"

I groaned. He just didn't know when to let up. "Huh. I never realized that."

"The whole coven is named after your family?"

"Guess so."

"What aren't you saying."

"Nothing. Give me a hand opening the garage doors? I want to let some fresh air into the place. It still smells like rubber and ash."

He nodded and walked over, hitting the button I hadn't noticed. I expected them to be manual pull chains, but they had electric motors. One opened. The other made a hideous grinding noise and he hit the other button to stop it.

"Well that didn't sound good," I said, grateful for the distraction from the coven name conversation.

"Yeah. Sounds like the chain slipped the motor. I'll go next door and get a ladder to take a look."

"It can wait. One door is good enough. I was serious about wanting you here to make introductions."

"That may not go as well as you think. Don't forget, they stopped wanting to have anything to do with me when I wouldn't give up questioning them about Rebecca's death. Hell, I think half of them thought I did it. You might want to let Jimmy or Dennis handle the introductions."

"If we don't deal with this, the coven will never be whole."

He opened his mouth to say something else, but Jimmy and Dennis walked through the open garage door. "Good timing, guys. I'll be right back. Gonna grab a ladder," he said and shot out the door before I could stop him.

"Everything okay?" Dennis picked up on the awkward situation.

"Yeah. He's afraid of being around the other coven members, I think."

"Don't blame him. Things were horrible for a while there. He was almost frantic to find Becca's killer. We all

84

understand that. It cut him a lot of slack. I think everybody is ready to put all that behind us now."

"Except for the one who killed Richie," I said solemnly. If it were a spell, it had to be one of the coven members.

Josie walked in carrying three boxes of donuts and two gallons of coffee. "Help," she said angrily.

"Shit." I strode forward and pulled the two gallons of coffee off the boxes of donuts.

"Thank you! It was only a couple of doors down. I didn't think they'd be that heavy..."

Dennis grabbed the boxes of donuts from her, leaving her with the bag of cups and condiments. "Where you want these?"

"Let's put it in the kitchen. Josie, come look."

"I'll give the chief a hand when he gets back," Jimmy interjected.

I nodded. "Want coffee?"

"I'll get it in a minute."

"I'll grab you one," Dennis told him and we headed for the kitchen.

"I was thinking about turning the kitchen into a small café-slash-coffee shop. Sandwiches and such. Whatever you can handle."

"It's perfect!" She practically ran around the commercial kitchen. She checked the appliances, but the stove didn't turn on.

"I called for water and electric. Didn't think about the gas. We might want to have someone come in and check everything before we turn it on."

"The water heater is probably gas, too. You might want to call right away, if you want hot water. I'll check it when I give Jimmy coffee. I'll take one for the chief, too."

"Thanks, Dennis."

I didn't even have to use my computer to find the utility number. There was a sticker on the vent hood with Danbur County Gas on it. It even had instructions for having the gas turned on. I made sure everything was off and made the call. They told me they'd have somebody out shortly.

I hung up. Dennis had just returned from delivering coffee and checking the water heater. "They'll be here soon," I told him.

"It's gas. The guys said thanks for the coffee. I'm going to go supervise them. Make sure nobody falls off the ladder."

"Well, they can come get donuts when they're hungry. Gimme cofffeee."

Josie poured me a cup and I inhaled its delicious aroma before taking a sip. "This is *good*. We're going to have competition."

"Not really. They literally serve coffee. No macchiatos, lattes, cappuccinos, or anything iced or frozen. We should be fine."

"*That's* why you volunteered to go. You were scoping out the competition!"

She blushed, which told me everything I needed to know. I swelled with pride. She was taking the business very seriously. I gave her a smile.

"I'm going to go check on the guys. Not that I don't trust Dennise, but there are ladders involved. This never ends well."

"I'm going to go check the rest of the place out. You wanna come?"

I shook my head. "I already did. I'm going to go supervise and see if anybody else shows up."

"Okay. You just wanna stare at asses on ladders. I see how you are."

"Holy shit. I didn't even think of that!" I fake ran toward the door and chuckled as Josie erupted into giggles behind me. As soon as I did clear the exit, I *did* walk a lot faster. Asses on ladders were always epic.

There were four hot guys in my garage. Dane had come over from next door, wearing his police uniform. "Hi, Dane."

"Hello, Dot. Nice place you have here."

"It will be. Coffee and donuts in the kitchen."

He smiled and took off, calling, "Thanks," over his shoulder.

"And you wonder why we make donut jokes," I told Chief standing on top of a very tall extension ladder. Jimmy *and* Dennis were holding the base.

"He's new. After twenty years, he'll be sick of them, too."

"How long have you been chief?" I realized I'd never asked.

"Five years. Been on the force for twenty."

"How old are you?"

"Fifty."

"Oh, my Lady. You're a baby?"

"I am not. I'm just not old."

"How old are you two?" I shifted my conversation to the other two.

"Thirty-five," Jimmy said.

"Twenty-seven," Dennis answered.

I felt like an old maid, I was older than almost all three of them together. *And* I'd just moved out of my mother's house...

I decided to change the topic. "Well, how's it look?"

Chief looked down and shrugged. "The teeth were ground off the motor assembly. I magicked it back. Just trying to get the chain back over it."

"Be careful," I called up and stared at his ass, not wanting to waste the opportunity.

Jimmy noticed the direction of my gaze and poked me between the ribs. I blushed and wiggled my eyebrows at him. "Perv," he whispered.

"Would you prefer it if I were up on the ladder?"

He nodded vigorously.

Dennis said, "Please?"

"So, you're telling me it's okay for you to stare at *my* ass, but I'm not allowed to look? It makes me a pervert if I do?"

"Yeah. Pretty much."

"That's kind of chauvinistic."

"It's not chauvinistic. It's territorial. I wouldn't mind at all if it were me up on the ladder and you were staring."

"Oh." I was a little shocked at his openness. "So, you want me to look at your ass?"

"Anytime you want."

"I'll keep that in mind. What about you, Dennis? Do you want me to stare at your ass, too?"

He nodded and smiled before blushing. He was just too damn cute. I sighed. I was gonna have my hands full with those two. I wasn't necessarily done talking about asses either...

I moved around Jimmy and pretended to be focusing on Chief's work, not his posterior. Reaching down I pinched his left butt cheek. He looked behind him, but didn't swat my hand away. I did it again and a soft chuckle escaped his lips.

Dennis looked over, but I was blocking his view and pretending nothing was going on. I slipped my hand in my front pocket and looked around the garage. He shrugged and focused on the chief again. I slipped my hand out of my pocket and instead of pinching, ran it over Jimmy's butt cheek, palming it and giving it a gentle squeeze. He shifted his stance. I took a step forward and ran my fingers over his hip, just above his jeans. Turning a bit, I started to reach for the front of his jeans... I stopped myself just short and started blushing furiously. I couldn't believe I had almost gone that far. Jimmy was staring at my hand. I could visibly see him swelling in his jeans.

"I'm hungry. I might not be a cop, but I like donuts." I pulled my hand back and headed toward the kitchen, leaving him standing there in the open with an inflation problem.

"Keep the chief safe, boys."

"I think I got it," Chief called down and started descending the ladder.

I stopped and turned around to see the result. They moved the ladder out of the way and Dennis hit the button. The motor whined to life, sparked, and died in a puff of smoke.

"Maybe not." The chief looked chagrined.

"It's okay. I'll have the GC replace the damn thing. Not sure if I'm keeping the doors, anyway. I'll probably put the entrance there."

"Sorry."

"Seriously. Don't be. One door should be enough for ventilation now. If you three want to start restoring things, I'd appreciate it. I'll go start looking for contractors. Let me know when everyone is here."

"Give Johnson Brothers a call. They're reliable and honest."

"Thanks, Jimmy," I said warily. Unsure if he was serious or making a Johnson joke...

"Seriously. They're the biggest contractors in Cedar Falls," he added, answering my question. Dennis nodded.

"I think they might be the only contractors left in the area," Chief added.

"I'll give them a Google." I opened the door to the living area and headed for the kitchen. Josie was talking to a blonde woman, casually drinking coffee and eating a donut.

"Hello?" I slipped into the kitchen, making my greeting a question.

"You must be Dot." She set her coffee down and held out her hand.

"I am," I replied and shook it gently. She was a wisp of a woman. If she were taller than five-feet it would have been a small miracle. No pun intended. She couldn't have weighed more than eighty or ninety pounds either, but she didn't look like a child. If anything, she looked elven. Her ears were even *slightly* pointed.

"I'm Candace. One of the coven. The chief said you were new to the area and needed some help. Josie," she paused and gave my friend a smile," just filled me in. Welcome to Cedar Falls."

I relaxed. "Thanks, Candace. And thanks for the help. Sorry, we were in the garage trying to fix one of the doors." I took in the rest of her. She was wearing denim overalls that were two sizes too large, but not too tall for her slight frame. If she'd been wearing a jacket, she'd taken it off in the warmer kitchen, leaving her midriff bare beneath the overalls. Her billowy half-shirt had long sleeves and were red and white striped. She was actually quite adorable. I wanted to pat her head.

"I'll go say hi," she said and pointed at the door.

"Yep, just go straight across the hall. Entrance to the garage is there."

"Thanks."

She disappeared, and I turned toward Josie. "I thought she was a kid at first."

"I know. She came in and I didn't even notice her for a minute. She's *quiet*."

"What were you talking about?"

"The area, why we were here. You."

"Hope you had nice things to say."

"Yeah. I made some up."

"Good."

"Wouldn't want to scare her on the first day."

"True story."

"Don't eat her."

"That's your department."

"Oh, my Lady. I can't believe you went there." She busted out laughing.

"That's my line."

"Stop!" She had wrapped her arms around her stomach, laughing. "I'm going to pee."

"That's too kinky. Even for me."

She ran to the bathroom. My work there was done. I headed for the front door, wanting to grab a breath of fresh air and get the smell of woodsmoke and rubber hose out of my nose. I should have grabbed my jacket. It was getting colder instead of warmer. My breath fogged in the morning air. A minivan passed by me and turned into the parking lot beside the store. Four people were inside and waved as they passed. I guessed they were more coven members.

I guessed right. Two youngish-looking couples came around the corner, chatting as they walked.

"Hello," I called out to them.

"You must be Dorothy?"

"It's actually Dorothea, but I absolutely *abhor* that name. Call me Dot, please."

"I'm David. This is my wife, Connie."

I shook their hands. "Nice to meet you both. Thanks for coming today."

"I'm Blake and this is Cindy. We're the Connors."

"Hello, Connors. Thank you for coming, too. If you want to head inside, there's coffee and donuts. Everybody else is in the garage, I believe."

"Thank you!"

"Wow. You are gorgeous," Connie managed to say nervously.

"Um. Thanks?" I didn't know what else to say.

"I mean it. Why did you move here? You should be a model in the city or something."

"I hate cities. Grew up in a small town like this. And I'm not that pretty."

"I've told you a million times you are," Josie said behind me.

I moved out of the way. "Everyone, this is my best friend, Josie. Josie, this is David, Connie, Blake, and Cindy," I said proudly, remembering their names. I usually sucked at them.

"Nice to meet you all."

"Come in. Get out of the cold."

We headed into the kitchen, letting them grab some coffee and food. Chief came in and nodded to everyone. "Hi, guys," he said nervously.

"Hey, Bill!" They sounded happy to see him. I didn't understand his hang-up. Blake even gave him a brotherly hug. The women kind of gushed, I noticed. Amusedly. Maybe jealously.

He turned to me. "We have one more on the way. Jason. Dwight can't make it. He's got a shift at the factory this morning. I'll introduce you to him later."

"Sounds good. As soon as Jason gets here, we can get started. Want some more coffee?"

"Please."

I grabbed his cup and filled it from the box of joe. "Here you go." I managed to splash some on my hand. It was still hot enough to burn. I wiped it off on the back of my leggings.

"Thanks, Dot."

"You're welcome, Chief."

He took his cup and headed back toward the garage. The rest of them sort of followed him. I heard woops and greetings through the closed door and smiled. It was good for all of them to be together again. I wondered how long it had been.

I turned my computer to face me and did a quick search for the Johnson Brothers. I wasn't sure if they'd be open on a Saturday, but I gave it a shot. Someone picked up on the third ring.

"Johnson Brothers."

"Hi. My name's Dot. I just bought the firehouse downtown. By the police station?"

"Yep. I know it. You're looking to make it into a bookstore."

He didn't even phrase it in question form. He'd be horrible at Jeopardy. "Um. Yeah. I see you know all about it."

Laughter rattled through the line. "Welcome to Cedar Falls. You're looking for a general contractor to do the work?"

"Yes. A bunch of us are...here doing some restorations, but I'm looking to have a bunch more work done. I was wondering if you could stop by sometime in the future and take a look, give me an estimate?"

"I'll actually be down there in a few minutes. I'll stop by."

Panic seized my chest, but then a plan formulated in my head. I'd hold the meeting and restoration party after he looked around. It shouldn't take him long to get an idea. It would be a while before he got to work on the job, anyway. "Sounds good. I'm the brunette in a ponytail."

"And you'll probably be the only person in town I don't recognize."

"There's that, too. So, yeah. Look for the stranger."

"Will do. See you shortly."

"Thanks."

The line clicked dead. He was a man of few words. Hopefully his work was as efficient as his conversational skills. I practically ran into the garage to let everybody know we were about to have a visitor.

I nearly hit Jimmy in the face with the door. "Sorry. Contractor will be here in a minute!"

He looked over his shoulder. "Guys, Freddie's stopping by to give Dot an estimate. Act normal," he said and started laughing before passing me and heading into the kitchen.

I felt like an idiot.

I sighed and followed him, fully intending to swat him in the head for making *me* feel like an idiot...

His lips caught mine as soon as I got in the room. Nearly screaming in surprised, I realized who was kissing me and I leaned into it, wrapping my arms around his back and closing my eyes. Jimmy kissed like a Greek god. I melted in his arms. It had been far too long since I'd felt anything that

93

remarkably good. His tongue warred with mine for dominance until he pulled back and captured my lower lip between his teeth.

I breathed out in exquisite bliss. I could feel myself getting wet as the pleasure raced through me. Until he let go of me and started pouring himself some more coffee. I stared at him in absolute horror as I realized it was a retaliation tactic for teasing him on the ladder.

"You sonofabitch." I couldn't help but laugh.

He shot me a slow seductive wink and blew me a kiss.

"I'll let you live. For now."

"Hey, at least I didn't rub your ass and leave you pitching a tent."

"Had I been pitching a tent, you'd have been horrified."

"Hmmm. True." He gasped in shock and looked down at the front of my leggings. "Whew."

"At least I didn't make you squishy," I said and turned around, walking a little funny and leaving him cackling in the kitchen.

"What's wrong?" Chief asked as I nearly collided with him.

"Spilled something on the front of my pants. Going to dry off," I kind of lied and went to walk around him. He grabbed my shoulders. "Here, I have a towel," he said and yanked a hand towel that had been hanging out of his back pocket.

What kind of fucking boy scout carries around a towel?

"Er. Um. It soaked my underwear. I'll just run to the bathroom."

"Oh. *Oh!* Sorry." He stepped back and looked up at the ceiling.

I should have just taken the towel from him and wiped off my lady parts. That would have taught him a very valuable lesson.

94

Chapter 10

"If we knock out this wall, you'll give yourself a bit more room for bookcases and blocking off the back of the storefront. You'll have to make this entrance to the café a little bigger, but I'd leave that open. We can expand the front of the entrance after we remove the garage doors. That way you can have a double entrance. You'll thank me in the middle of winter."

I looked up at Freddy Johnson. He stood almost six-and-a-half feet tall. His "little" brother, Teddy, was an inch taller. Appearance aside, they completely shocked me with not only their knowledge, but their ability to really picture the design I had in mind. "Let's go with that, then."

He nodded and jotted down some more notes in a brand-new spiral notebook. He even wrote BOOKSTORE on the front of it in sharpie. The pages had been filled with elaborate hand drawn sketches of the building from all sides and detailed notes of each room and what needed to be done.

"What kind of wood do you want for the bookcases?"

"I have no idea."

"I'd go with something dark. If you want to keep the price down, we can still use decent wood and stain it. Bookstores should not be bright and cheery. I'd go with minimal illumination. Probably some high hats in the ceiling and focused LED spots for the shelves."

It was official. I was lost. However, competence exuded from every pore of both of the brothers. Few people *found* their calling in life. These two had been born to be contractors. I decided to trust their instincts. I could always blame Jimmy for recommending them if they screwed me or did a shitty job.

"Tell you what, gentlemen. Do this and do it right. You came *highly* recommended. Build my bookstore. Let me know how much it's going to set me back and I'll tell you yay or nay. Sound good?"

"You betcha," Freddy said, earning a definite nod from Teddy.

"I won't even ask you for a ballpark now. I'll let you plan and check pricing on materials before you give me an estimate."

"Bless you, child. Nothing worse than giving a ballpark and then coming back with an estimate, then having to listen to the but you saids. We won't cut corners but keep it as cheap as possible."

"Thanks, guys. Let me know."

"Give us a call on Wednesday. We should have everything ready for you by then." Teddy handed me a business card.

"Will do. Thanks!"

They turned around and left through the open door. I watched the massive middle-aged men climb up into the dually parked on the street.

"How much?" Chief asked as they pulled away.

"They'll give me an estimate on Wednesday. Tell everybody thanks for their help, but we don't need to do anything. They're going to tear this place up anyway. It would be a waste of magic."

"You tell them. They're ready for our meeting."

I sighed and steeled my nerves. I'd never liked speaking in front of groups. It's one of the reasons I never wanted to be high priestess of any coven. We headed into the bunk room. Someone had produced enough folding chairs for everyone. They'd been arranged in a circle. Two empty seats sat open by the door. Chief led the way and took the one to the left. I sat and took a sip of my cold coffee, wetting my mouth.

"Greetings, Coven of the Gold Moon."

"Greetings, Lady," they responded in unison, as they would have to a high priestess. I let it go. I had called the meeting. That was all the ceremony we were standing on.

"I just wanted to talk to you all. There are a few items that need discussion. First and foremost, thank you for having me and my friend, Josie, in your coven. We were pleasantly surprised to find so many wonderful witches quietly living in our new community."

I bowed. They smiled and returned my bow. It seemed a little funny with all of us sitting in metal folding chairs, but we did it anyway.

"Secondly, I wanted to thank you all for not only offering your magic to help me restore the firehouse but agreeing to this meeting. The former will not be needed, however. The contractors I just met with have plans to tear this place apart and basically rebuild it from the ground up to suit the needs of the bookstore. Still, I appreciate your help."

They nodded and smiled.

"The last issue is a little more delicate. As most of you know, Richie passed away the other day. What some of you might not know is that magic was most likely the cause of his death. Chances are he was murdered. By another witch."

They exploded. I held up my hand and they calmed, their questions dying off. "Do not get me wrong. I am simply stating the most probable cause of his death. I am *not* accusing anyone in this room. Especially after meeting all of you, I do not think any one of you did this. The chief *may* have some questions for you. Please answer them, but this will not turn into–and please pardon the euphemism–a witch hunt. That leads me into the reason I have told all of you this. It came to my attention that you all have not been in the practice of using personal shields."

They shot me curious looks. I sighed and continued. "This isn't a wise practice. Shields are not only there for your protection, they are for the protection of the mortals around you. It is all about intent. Intent infused with will and magic becomes reality. It only takes a moment for anger or desire to blend the three into a spell. Please, *please*, work on maintaining your shields at *all* times. Even when you sleep. It will become ingrained on your will and you will reach a point where you don't even have to think about it. Shields won't protect you from everything, but it might give you enough time to run or retaliate."

They nodded. Dane raised his hand.

"Yes?" I said, curiously.

"Why didn't your shield protect you from a binding spell?"

"That's a good question. What is the first thing that you do when you cast your shield?"

He thought about it for a moment. "Ground it?"

"Yes! You ground your magic. Now where did the bindings come from?"

"The ground at your feet." He understood as soon as he spoke.

I continued. "Shields can stop the immediate blast of fire. They can stop even the most effective scrying. Lightning and psychological attacks will be pushed into the earth at your feet. Windborne and water attacks will flow around you. Earth attacks however, your best bet is to attack back and hope your attack hits first. Now do you all understand the importance of shields?"

"Why did you say they would protect those around you?"

Seriously? Were these witches taught nothing?

"Sorry. I do not know what you were or were not taught. A spell is a binding of your intent, will, and magic. It's why we predominantly use the words of a secondary language. I prefer Irish. Chief uses Welsh. Josie uses Latin. We say the words of our intent, picture the outcome using our will, and then push our magic into the spell, which acts as a catalyst, binding the three of them together and making it happen. Let's say you were married. You came home one day and found your spouse in bed with their secretary. Anger flares inside you. You want your spouse to just die. At the same moment you picture them, lying dead in the bed. The anger also causes a flare in your magic. That one moment of anger becomes a spell, even without the canting. By the time you realized what happened, your spouse is dead, the secretary is screaming, and you realized just how badly you fucked up.

"That's why it's important to have shields on you all the time. When shielded, the caster actually has to picture piercing the shield without destroying it in the spell or it just gets grounded."

Nods of understanding and clarity, even some shock, met my speech. I wish I could take credit for the wonderful analogy, but it had been passed down to me from my mother, and to her from her mother going back who knows how far. It was scary but accurate. I wondered which of my ancestors had learned the lesson the hard way.

"Any other questions?"

"Will you be our high priestess?"

The question, while not unexpected, tore my heart a little. It was the last–the very last–thing I wanted. Most of them knew this. Some did not. I sighed and stood. "I don't want to be a high priestess." The looks of disappointment on *all* their faces opened the wound in my heart a little more. "I ran away. My mother is due to step down as high priestess in the future. I was supposedly destined to step up as her replacement as the time came. Then I found the itch to move away too irresistible to resist. I followed it to this place. I've seen your broken town. It hurts my heart to see what it could be and what it is. My Ashville lives in symbiosis with the witch community and thrives. I think this might be why your town is suffering." I held up my hand. "I'm sure the economy and other factors contribute to this disarray, but I know we are playing a part of it, as well. *If* the lot of you can swear to me that we will work together for the benefit of the town and the people in it, I will step in and be your *temporary*," I stressed the word with every ounce of stress I possessed, "high priestess. If the Lady will have me."

The applause of the eleven around me threatened to deafen everyone in the room. I found myself wiggling my fingers in my ears when they were done. I gave them a wan smile in thanks. On the inside, I wanted to curl up in fetal position and cry.

What the hell was I thinking. I don't want to do this. Thankfully, it's only temporary…

"How do we know if she's worthy?" All eyes turned to on one of the witches I hadn't met before.

He must be Jason…

"Jason." Jimmy hissed his name.

"No. It's an honest question," I supplied in his defense. "No high priestess may be anointed without the blessing of the Lady. We'll perform the ceremony. If it not be the Lady's will, I will still join your coven, just not as your priestess."

He nodded, seemingly satisfied with my response.

"Any other questions?"

Eleven heads shook.

"Good, if someone is close to… What is the missing one's name?"

"Dwight."

"If someone could pass along all the info to Dwight, I would greatly appreciate it. At least until I have a chance to talk to him myself."

"I will," Jason said firmly.

"Thanks," I said a little warily. I wasn't getting the best of vibes from Jason. He was handsome enough, with thick waves of dirty blond hair. His eyes were a gorgeous blue, too. His face was a little too angular, though. It made him seem hard and uncaring. Looks aside, it was his demeanor that ruffled my feathers.

He nodded.

Chief stood and spoke. "Is everyone free Sunday night?"

Everyone shrugged and nodded.

"Good. Gather in the north woods. You know the location. Get there around eleven-thirty so we can ask the Lady's blessing."

"Lady's Blessing," everyone said in unison and stood.

I didn't respond in kind. I wasn't the high priestess yet. I did smile, glad the meeting was over. My anxiety was at its peak. I needed to go home, have a bath, and a nap.

"Told you so," Josie whispered behind me.

"Shut your face up. I can't believe I agreed."

"The Lady's hand doth guide..."

"The friend doth talk too much."

Josie giggled and pinched my back. "I'm going to go get another coffee. Where we heading?"

"Home. I need some therapy."

"I'll meet you downstairs."

"'Kay."

I took the time to say goodbye to everyone, saving my trio for last. They pushed back toward the corner of the room, letting everyone have the chance. When the Connors finally exited, the four of us were finally alone.

"So, what do you think of everyone?" Chief sounded a little afraid of my answer.

"They all seem very nice." It dawned on me that Jason hadn't said goodbye. I had a feeling he didn't like me. I glanced back at the door. "Maybe not Jason."

Jimmy chuckled. "Yeah. He and Dwight are a little different, but once you get to know them..."

"They're nice guys?"

"No. They're still pricks, but you can tolerate them," Dennis answered.

I looked at the three of them. "What do I do now? I don't want to do this..."

"It's not too late to back out," Chief said sadly. "It would be a waste. You were amazing. Even I didn't know hardly any of that. I guess I got lucky with my binding spell."

"Yes, you did." I laughed.

"That sounds kinky," Jimmy said with an evil smile. I thought I heard a note of jealousy in his voice, though. Maybe something else.

"If it weren't in the police station with Dane watching, it might have been." I decided to throw a little fuel on the fire. I owed Jimmy big time. I was still squishy.

He opened his mouth to say something else, but closed it and gave me a little grin. "Guess our night out at the bar is on hold. Not that I mind."

"Oh shit. I forgot. Sorry guys, raincheck."

"No hardship on our part. We're looking forward to it immensely."

I shot Jimmy a questioning look.

Chief coughed.

"What?"

"I think he's looking forward to seeing you skyclad..."

"Oh. Well, I hope you three enjoy the view." I meant it. Being naked in front of the coven wasn't something I minded. I'd been raised in a powerful coven. Most, if not all, rituals were skyclad. As long as I didn't have to speak in front of everyone, I'd be fine.

I hated to even have the thought, but I would definitely be happy seeing the three of them naked in the moonlight. Daylight. Spotlight. Bedroom light... Whatever.

"Well, I have a mountain of laundry to get done," Chief said, gave me a little bow, and headed for the door.

"See ya, Chief."

He paused a moment and sighed before continuing on.

"Are you ever gonna call him Bill?"

I turned to Jimmy. "Probably not."

Chapter 11

"Are you ready to go? Chief is here."

Nodding at Josie, I fastened my cloak around my neck with the large pin my mother had gifted to me on my sixteenth year. I patted it and pushed away the homesick feeling that tried its best to settle in my chest.

"Yeah." I twirled, my cloak flaring around me, showing off the naked flesh beneath.

"Do that again. It was kind of hot."

"Shut up. You see me naked all the time."

"Yeah, but it's hotter with the cloak."

"You're weird."

"No. You're just hot."

I decided to ignore her. These were the arguments I would never win. I padded softly through the living room and grabbed a pair of ankle-high sandals from the front closet. Chief whistled when he saw me.

Sitting down on the couch, I noticed he was wearing jeans and a button-down shirt. "Um. Aren't you a little over dressed?"

"It's thirty-three degrees out there. I'll strip at the clearing. Safer for Captain Nightstick that way."

"You did not just call your dick Captain Nightstick."

"Um. Force of habit. It wasn't me who came up with that name…"

I let it go. I didn't want, or need, to know. "Do you have all the components and implements?"

"Yep. They're already at the clearing."

"Do you want a drink?"

"No. I'm fine. You sound like you could use one, though."

"You have no idea."

"Why are you nervous? You know this is going to go fine."

"That's what I'm afraid of. Moved four states away to *not* have to do this. And here I am. What am I doing?"

"Three states."

"We drove through Maryland for like ten minutes. Four."

"Fine four. Go have a drink."

I sighed, heading for the kitchen. I opened the door of the fridge and popped open a beer. "*Bheith fuar,*" I whispered, chilling it before it reached my lips. It went down like bitter truth. I coughed and repeated the procedure.

Three beers later and I wasn't ready to bolt.

"Slow down there, frat boy."

I looked at the trio of bottles on the counter in front of me. "Shush. It's medicine."

"Uh huh. Look. I'm not doing this to get you to call me Bill."

"What?" I turned around as his arms wrapped around me.

Turning my head, I pressed it against his chest. His heartbeat calmed me a little bit more, so did his warmth and his scent. I let out the breath I'd been holding without realizing it.

"Thanks, Bill."

"You seemed like you needed it. Want me to let go?"

"No. Not yet. We still have a few more minutes."

"Okay."

He rocked side to side for a minute. I rubbed my cheek against the rough material of his shirt, my arms wrapping around his waist. It had the unfortunate side-effect of opening my cloak. There I stood in the middle of my kitchen, holding a fully clothed man while I was butt naked. I don't think he would have appreciated my asking him to strip, so I let it go.

"Thanks," I whispered and stepped back, letting the cloak fall into place. Not before he smiled in admiration.

"Come on. We'd better get going."

"You riding with us?"

"No. You're riding with me."

"Cuff me before you toss me in the back?" I asked hopefully.

"You have serious issues."

That made me laugh and took the last of the edge off the butterflies threatening to shank me and escape through the gaping wound.

I sat in the front of the Cherokee and Josie got to ride in the back. It took ten minutes to get to the clearing. We were almost late thanks to my nerves. We made it with just a few minutes to spare. I hadn't realized the clearing was that far into the woods, but luckily there was a trail the jeep could follow.

Ten witches stood around a blazing fire and no one was wearing a cloak. We were going to be holding many winter ceremonies. I'd put an order in for a bunch of them and make them gifts for yule.

Chief parked next to the other two vehicles. I guess they believed in carpooling at least, and I gave silent thanks I'd let Chief drive. My Soul wouldn't have made it over the trail.

We got out of the vehicle and walked into the clearing. Even with the fire it was near freezing. We stepped over the salt line someone had used to cast the circle around the entire clearing. I reached down and gently touched my finger to it, canting, "*Coinnigh muid te!*"

The fire began glowing brightly and the air inside the circle warmed. Gooseflesh smoothed as I moved into the throng of witches. Chief nodded his thanks and began removing his clothing.

It was improper to stare, so I smiled at everyone gathered. I moved to the altar by the fire. I also smiled at the scian, goblet of salt, a switch of willow, and bowl of purified water. All of which had been thrice blessed beneath the moon that night.

"Ready," Chief called over to me.

I unhooked the pin at my neck and set it before me upon the altar. Raising my arms to the sky, I let the cloak fall free and gather at my feet as I gazed to the moon and chanted:

Blessed be our Mother
We pray for you this night
Guide our coven forward
And shine upon us light
Our priestess has been lost
We ask of you our right
Let your wisdom guide us
And help us with our plight
Show the one you favor
And bless her with your might

The breeze, warm as it was from the spell, stilled completely. The circle flared and coalesced all around us in a miasma of light. I picked up the scian and parted the flesh of my finger, letting the blood fall into the bowl of purified water. The coven circled the alter, each member pausing before me. I drew blood from them and added it to the bowl. With each drop it began to glow brighter and brighter. As the thirteenth drop fell, it chimed like the toll of a bell.

The light around us flared again, nearly blinding us in its intensity. My body went rigid and I found myself unable to move. I was forced from my very flesh as the Lady filled me completely.

Standing inside the circle, next to myself, I looked down at my hand and could see the ground through it. My spirit had been forced from my body.

Gazing up at my very own face, the Lady gave me a small patient smile. "Be at ease daughter. I merely wish to speak."

I bowed and made to step back, but she reached out with her hand and held my spirit fast by her side.

"I grant this one the title of high priestess. Show her all the love you would show me. Gone is the Coven of the Gold Moon. Its days are long past. From this day forward, thou art the Coven of the First Moon..."

There was a collective gasp as the Lady held up her hand and anointed my forehead. A faint sliver of a moon flared with light and then fainted from view. The goddess smiled and left my body, drawing me back in.

The wind picked back up and I dropped to the floor of the forest, neatly landing on my cloak. Josie rushed forward, and I held up my hand. I was fine. I just needed a moment.

"Well, that was something," Chief said, standing above me.

"That wasn't supposed to happen, I don't think. Never before has a coven been renamed. I've never heard of the Lady making an appearance either..." Josie sounded frightened and amazed at the same time.

"The coven wasn't renamed. We were born anew. You heard her," I explained to Josie.

"We didn't want that."

I looked at Jason. He was beginning to be a pain in my ass. Already. "I didn't ask for it to be so. It was the Lady's decision. If you want to question her wisdom, please do so at your own discretion and not while I'm around. Thank you."

"But–"

"Jason!" Dwight, or I assumed it was Dwight, silenced him with his terse tone. "Respect."

Jason looked like he still wanted to argue, but he shut his mouth and stepped back a little. I nodded my thanks to Dwight.

As I made a move to get to my feet, Chief and Josie each grabbed an arm. "Is it hot in here or is it just me?"

"No. It's very warm," Chief said and I noticed his nakedness for the first time as I stood up.

Holy shit. Now I know how he earned his nickname...

I blinked and focused my attention anywhere but there. It just happened to focus on the coven standing before me. Some of them looked like they were about to cry. Some of them looked afraid. But the thing I noticed most was the energy swirling around each and every one of them. I could see the soft glow of their power inside them as well as their shields around them. They were beautiful.

"Well. Greetings, Coven of the First Moon."

"Greetings, Lady." They bowed. All of them. Even Jason.

Above us, the soft sizzling noise of snowflakes melting against the dome of light surrounding us drew our attention upward.

∞ ∞ ∞

I groaned as I slipped between my nice warm covers.

Why couldn't the itch have pulled us to Florida?

A soft knock at my door snapped me out of my wishful thinking. "I'm awake, Josie," I called out softly.

The door opened, and Josie padded softly into my room wearing her pink terrycloth robe. "Hey."

"Hey, you."

"Mind if I sleep in here?"

I laughed. Whenever Josie got freaked out about anything, she didn't like to be alone. We slept in the same bed quite often. "Sure."

I turned on my side and closed my eyes. She could be the big spoon.

"So. Um. That was something..."

"What?" I decided to pretend it wasn't that big of a deal. Maybe she would actually get some sleep.

"Don't you dare 'what' me. You know damn well what I'm talking about. You were visited. By the *goddess*."

"Oh, that. Yeah. She was much nicer than I was expecting."

"Dot, do you know how often that happens? Try *never*. I know. I broke down and called my mother."

"You what?" Ignoring the fact I was naked under the covers, I sat straight up and stared down at her incredulously.

"Called my mom."

"Why the fuck would you do that?"

"Well, I figured if I told her that we were fine and joined a coven, she might actually start saying something to me other than, 'If you don't get your delinquent ass back home, I'm disowning you.'"

"Josie, while I appreciate the fact that you are having difficulty dealing with your mother, now that you've hung up with her, what do you think the first thing she's going to do is?"

She thought about it for a moment. "Um. Call your mother?"

"Precisely. After she greets my mother, what do you then think the first thing she's going to tell her is?"

"That you were visited by the Lady?"

"And what do you think my mother is going to do?"

"Um. Call you?"

On cue, my phone started ringing. I kept staring at Josie as I blindly reached over to the nightstand and brought the phone over to stick in Josie's face. "Tell me, Josie. Who might that be calling me at this hour?"

"Um. Chief."

"What?" I looked at the phone. It really did say Chief across the screen.

I swiped it open to answer it.

109

"Hello?"

"Sorry. I know it's really late. There's been another murder…"

Chapter 12

I pulled my car up to the address the chief had texted me on the way over. I'd also ignored fourteen phone calls from my mother. I may not have been right on cue, but I was right. I promised myself to give Josie bunny ears when I got home. I'm not talking about holding my fingers above her head. I was going make that shit grow right out the top of her skull. She deserved nothing less.

My car skidded to a slight stop on the snowy road. We got snow in Virginia, but not much. I wasn't used to driving on slick roads. At least I didn't crash into the back of the coroner's truck. That would have been embarrassing.

The chief was waiting for me in the doorway. "Nice stop."

"Not in the mood. Was it a witch?"

His solemn nod told me all I needed to know.

"Who?"

"Dane."

"No! They killed a cop?"

"Yes. We need to figure out who is doing this and why. Quickly."

"Let me see the body."

"Herb waited for you."

"Herb? I forgot he was the coroner. He's human."

"But after being the coroner for twenty-seven years, he figured things out pretty quickly. Feel free to talk in front of him. He knows not to ask questions."

"Okay."

Herb was sitting on Dane's couch, the body on the floor by the door. He had fallen backwards. Whoever killed him had done it from the door. "Hey, Herb."

"Hi, Dot. Are you?"

I nodded. "Yep."

"I should have figured that out from the beginning. Welcome to the party."

"Next time I'll bring beer."

I crouched down next to Dane and said a silent prayer to the Lady. "May you be reborn into a better life."

He wasn't burned like Richie. Someone had slashed him with a knife across is throat. He was lying in a puddle of blood and I looked up at the wall. It had painted a red rainbow across the white paint and front window.

"Could a spell have cut him like this?"

I leaned closer to the body. I could feel some residual magics, but their intent had been to burn, not to cut. "It could have, but it wasn't. Whomever did this to him had tried to burn him. I can feel the spell. When it didn't work, they slashed his throat."

"You can feel all that?"

"Yes. But at least we know one thing."

"What?"

"It wasn't a member of our Coven. They would have known that their spell wouldn't have worked and started with the knife."

"Or they wanted it to *look* like it wasn't someone in the coven."

His logic made sense. "Or that. Yeah."

"Thanks, Herb. You can bag him up now."

"Okay, Chief."

"I'll be out front," I told him. "Night, Herb."

"Night, Dot."

I walked through the front door and sighed, crossing my arms and leaning against one of the porch columns. We were missing something. Something simple. I could feel it.

Chief came out and leaned against the other column. He didn't look sad, he looked angry. "You couldn't tell who cast the spell?"

"Not today. Maybe in ten years when I learn the feel of each and every person's magic in our coven, I could. But, not yet. Assuming it even was one of them. I feel like we're missing something easy."

"Nothing's easy when it comes to murder."

"Murder is for some people. It's too easy."

"I meant solving it. Killing *is* easy."

"You gonna be okay? Were the two of you close?"

"Worked together for ten years. Knew him longer than that. I talked him into becoming a cop. Figured it was safe enough in a small town like this. Guess I was wrong."

"Stupid time to ask, but what did he have in common with Richie?"

At least he thought about it for a minute before shaking his head. "I haven't got a clue. Maybe the murders are just random. Who knows."

"You're afraid to start questioning the coven again." I didn't ask, I said it.

He looked me in the eye and nodded slowly.

"I can be there with you if you want."

"Technically this falls under police business, not coven."

"I know. I'm not stepping on your toes, was just offering some moral support."

"That's very…kind. Thanks, Dot."

"You're welcome…Bill."

"Hey. I didn't hug you."

"You want to?"

"I could sort of use one right now. You don't mind?"

"Not at all."

He stepped a little closer and opened his arms instead of enveloping me in them. I met him halfway and wrapped my arms around his stomach, pressing my head against his chest. He even kissed the top of my head. Nothing more. We just stayed like that until Herb carted the body out the front door. He was the first to let go.

"Thanks."

"Anytime."

"Well, you better get home. It's getting colder out, and we're supposed to get a few inches of snow tonight. I'll see you tomorrow, Dot. Thanks for your help."

"You gonna be okay?"

"Eventually. I'm going home to have a very stiff drink and get some sleep."

"Okay. Call me if you need anything." I padded down the concrete steps and got in my car. Starting it up, I blasted the heat to dispel the chill I felt in my bones that had nothing to do with the weather. Getting back into my bed sounded better and better.

There was a strange car in my driveway when I pulled in. Warily, I got out and headed to the front door. I pulled my key out and nearly screamed when I noticed the man on the front porch. Luckily, I recognized Jimmy before I belted one out.

"Hey," he mumbled tiredly.

"Hey, yourself. You okay?"

"Lil drunk, but I'll live."

"Where's Dennis?"

"He pulled an extra shift. Left me all by my lonesome."

"How did you survive?"

"Bad choice of words. Heard about Dane."

"Yeah. He seemed like a nice guy."

"Who's doing this, Dot? Why?"

"Come inside. We'll talk. I'll make you some coffee."

He nodded and picked himself up off my concrete stoop. I walked up the stairs and patted his shoulder before fumbling the lock open. The smell of beer wafting off Jimmy was almost overwhelming.

"How many did you have?"

"Just a couple or twelve."

"No wonder you reek. Go take a shower. I'll loan you some sweats."

"Sorry. You sure?"

"I'm sure. I'll put a pot of coffee on. You can use the shower in the master bath."

"Thanks."

"Did you drive here?"

"Yeah."

I didn't hold back. I swatted him upside the head as I let him through the doorway. "Do it again and I will leave a scar. Got it?"

"Yes, ma'am."

I sighed and closed the door behind me, letting him head off to the shower. I didn't know if Josie was still in my bed, and I didn't care. Let her be shocked. Lady knew, she deserved it.

I headed into the kitchen and put the coffee on. Josie came padding out of her room, rubbing her eyes. "Who you talking to?"

"Jimmy. He was on the front porch, drunk off his ass. He's in the shower sobering up."

"Oh. *Oh!* Good luck!" She winked and nearly skipped back into her room, lightly closing the door behind her.

"Yeah, right."

I waited in the kitchen while the coffee brewed. The *glug, glug, glug* was interrupted by a resounding *thud* coming from my bathroom. I ran in to check on the drunk. He was lying naked on the shower floor, rubbing his head and wincing in pain.

"You okay?"

"No," he said defeated.

"Can you stand?"

He sat up, rubbing the back of his head. "Maybe someday."

I laughed. "Lean forward, let me see."

He did as I told him, the spray of water parting his unruly hair. I fingered through it, ignoring the spray of water, and didn't find any cuts. He did have a nice lump, however.

"You're not bleeding. We'll take that as a win."

"Easy with the fingers, though. That smarts."

"Aww, big tough fireman gots a wump on his head?"

"You're gonna get a wump on your ass."

"Ooh. Kinky."

He chuckled and let his head lean forward, letting the hot water run down his neck and back. His skin was darker than mine, but not his ass. It nearly matched the white square tiles of the shower. It was very pretty.

"Would you help me up?"

"Did you finish showering yet?"

"No. I slipped getting in."

"Hang on."

I stepped back and pulled off my clothes. He had seen me naked earlier. I seriously doubted his ability to finish showering without breaking a bone or requiring stitches. At least that's what I told myself to justify getting into the shower with him.

I stepped in behind him and made sure I wasn't in a position to slip before hooking my arms under his. "Come on. I can't lift you. You have to *want* to stand. You can do it!"

"Har har. You're a real comedian," he said and worked himself to his knees, and then to his feet. As he stood up straight, his ass pressed into my naked front. "Um... Are you naked?"

"Yes. Don't turn around."

"But I saw you earlier."

"I know. But this is... Oh never mind. Turn around if you want. We're not twelve."

He didn't have to be asked twice. His eyes drank in my body. It was a little more intimate than standing in the grove in front of the entire coven. I could feel my nipples hardening even under the hot water, just from the weight of his gaze.

"Well?" I had to ask.

"You are beautiful."

I let my eyes drop a little lower. He wasn't as massive as Chief, but still impressive. I moved a little closer and reached over his shoulder to grab the bottle of shampoo. "Turn back around."

Surprisingly, he did as he was told.

I squirted some shampoo in my hand, set the bottle down on the floor and began lathering up his hair. He tilted his head back as I massaged it into his blondish locks.

"Do I get to wash your hair, too?"

"If you want. I'm telling you right now, we are not having sex tonight, so don't get your hopes up."

He started singing, "There's always tomorrow..." I even recognized the song from Rudolph. I slapped his ass with a sudsy palm.

"Hey. Be nice to the butt."

"If you're lucky. Turn around so I can rinse your head."

He turned around, his cock a little firmer than before. Its head slid across my skin. "Sorry," he mumbled, not sorry at all.

"Somebody's happy."

"Both of us."

I pressed up against him, running my fingers through his hair, the spray splashing down over his chest and onto me. He was trapped between my stomach and his. I fought very hard not to start moving up and down.

"That feels good," he managed to say coherently.

"Which part?"

"Both."

I got the rest of the shampoo out. "Do you use conditioner?"

"Who doesn't?"

"Fair enough. Turn back around."

He leaned over and gently kissed my lips before turning. I shuddered. He'd done exactly the right thing. If he had gone full force, I might have shoved him out of the shower...

I couldn't help it. While he was facing the other way, I slipped my fingers over my wet, and not from the shower, slit. I shuddered again and nearly came just from the swift touch. I don't think I'd ever been as turned on as I was in that moment.

Later, Dot.

I filled my hand with conditioner and rubbed my palms together. Jimmy tilted his head back and I worked my conditioner covered fingers through his hair, staring at his broad shoulders. I wanted to run my fingernails over them and down his back, but I maintained what little self-control I had left.

"Okay. Soap your bod and let me under the water so I can wash *my* hair."

"I don't get to do it?"

"Can I trust you to behave?"

"Absolutely...not, but I will get your hair washed."

I thought about saying no, but I really wanted him to wash it. There were few things on earth that felt quite as good as someone washing your hair for you. "Fine, but try to behave. Don't make me zap your happy parts."

He chuckled throatily as we squeezed by each other in the shower. I ran my auburn hair under the water and rinsed my face before backing up and letting him shampoo. He was more gentle than I would have expected, working the liquid into my hair and then massaging my scalp. I tilted my head back and enjoyed the myriad of sensations running through my body.

"Rinse time."

I turned around and let my hair fall into the flow of water behind me, tilting my head back. Jimmy stepped forward and reached behind me, rinsing my hair. His hardness pressed against my stomach again. I was getting dizzy with want. It'd definitely been way too long since I'd last had sex. I reached out to steady myself against his chest. The firmness of his muscles, the feeling of the water cascading over him, I pressed myself even closer. A small groan escaped his lips as his hips circled.

"I think you got all the shampoo out."

"You sure?"

"Pretty sure."

"Okay then. Turn around and I'll put the conditioner in."

I did as I was asked and wiped the water from my face, staring at the ceiling as he worked. Shampooing was much more fun. He reached around me and rinsed his hands in the stream of water before grabbing the body wash and loofa from the rack. I gasped as he began washing my neck.

He made small circles when he got to my shoulders and back. I closed my eyes and leaned my head forward when he moved on to my arms. I spread my legs a little as he gently washed my lower back, and I nearly bucked my hips when he began washing my ass cheeks.

I heard movement and a couple of thuds. I looked over my shoulder and Jimmy had knelt on the hard floor of the shower behind me. He began washing my feet and working his way up. I was panting by the time he got to my thighs.

"Turn around."

"I can't. That would be a horrible mistake," I managed to choke out.

"Fine."

I felt him stand behind me as I began to catch my breath. His arms slipped around me and the loofa began making lazy circles over my stomach. "That's not what I meant."

"I know. Tell me when to stop and I will."

"Promise?"

"Promise."

I rested my head back against his chest. His swollen cock nestled itself in the cleft of my ass. I'd never rinsed the soap away, he slid between easily, his height forcing him downward to my opening. He bumped against it, but never tried to force his way inside.

He dropped the sponge and used the lather on his hands to wash the rest of me. He started with my breasts, gently gliding underneath before circling up around the sides and over my rigid nipples. His palms slid over them and I whimpered against his jaw. His one hand stayed and played as his other snaked down over my stomach and began fondling the patch of hair just above my opening. My hips bucked on their own, trying to force his hand lower.

He kissed the side of my face as he let his middle finger slip in between my folds, over my clit and teasingly across my opening. His hand was slippery enough, but with my added moisture, he made lazy circles over my clit. All around, but never quite touching.

"Please," I whispered.

"Please what?"

"Make me come."

He moved his hand away and sluiced the shower water over me with the head, removing ever trace of suds. He backed me up against the wall and knelt down in front of me, staring at my pussy and darting his eyes to look up at me.

Lifting my leg, he put my foot on the edge of the shower, opening me before raking his tongue across me. For an eternity I rode his talented lips. I came twice before I had to push him away, too sensitive to continue.

I couldn't see straight.

"Holy shit."

"Not even gonna ask if you liked that."

"Smart man."

"Mind if I rinse the conditioner out of my hair?"

I'd completely forgotten. I blushed and moved out of the way, letting him back into the stream of water. Thankfully we hadn't run out of hot water, *yet*. He was rigid as he closed his eyes. I reached out, wrapped my hand around his length, and began jerking softly. He groaned.

Fair was fair. I dropped to my knees and kissed the tip. I looked up and he was staring at me as the water sprayed his neck and shoulders, blocking me. I could see the lust in his eyes as I slipped the tip into my mouth and ran my tongue along the underside.

"Dot. I'm not going to last long..."

I pulled the skin back, taut along the shaft and sucked him halfway in. It was as far as I could go before he hit the back of my throat. I wasn't an expert at this, not by a long shot. But for him, I would try. I sucked on him, actually enjoying the feeling of him in my mouth. His hips began bucking in rhythm. His breathing started getting heavier as he gave out little gasps of pleasure. I could feel his muscles tightening and after a few moments he reached out to steady himself.

"Dot. I'm cumming."

I thought about pulling away. I really hated the taste, but I didn't. I let him go in my mouth and continued jerking his shaft with my hand. He groaned softly and once finished, I pulled my mouth away and let his juice fall from my mouth and down the drain.

I stood up and got the shock of my life when he kissed me.

Chapter 13

The coffee was still hot, thank fuck.

I took a big swallow, burned the hell out of my tongue, and avoided any eye contact with Jimmy. As soon as we had exited the shower, I practically ran for my bathrobe.

Bad Dot. Bad, bad Dot.

He kept grinning at me over the top of his mug.

"You can stop that now," I said softly.

"What?"

"Flashing that shit-eating grin at me."

"I know not of which you speak."

"Keep it up and you're going to know the feeling of my foot in your ass."

"Now who's being kinky?"

My face flushed, completely on fire. "I hate you!"

"No. You don't."

"You're right. I don't. But that went a *lot* further than I'd intended. I was just trying to help your drunk ass in the shower."

"So, you stripped naked and climbed in there with me."

"Yep. I is a good Samaritan."

"You is. Thank you."

I blushed even harder. "How are you feeling?"

He smiled. "Completely *drained.*"

"Oh, my *God.* Will you stop. You're trying to make me blush to death."

"Nope. You just…"

"I just what?"

He set his mug down on the counter and put his hands on either side of it, looking me in the eyes. "You always seem so cool and collected. You take charge of every situation. You're just one of those people. Like you could run a multi-billion-dollar corporation or have dinner with a king and queen and not bat an eyelash. You're amazing. It's just nice seeing you a little flustered. Makes you seem more…human."

"Yeah, yeah." I waved my hand dismissively.

"Well, Dot. I must thank you again for *everything*. Especially the coffee. I should probably head home."

"Like hell you are. I'm sure you would still blow a dot-oh-eight. You're not driving."

"Ha! You just used the words dot and blow in the same sentence. You really can't say stuff like that and not expect me to make a joke."

I spit coffee.

I gave him the most horrified expression I could muster. He burst out laughing and nearly fell to the floor. Josie came running out of her room, took one look at the two of us, gave me a thumbs up, and waved goodbye.

I wanted to die.

"You can have the couch. I'm going to bed. One more joke and you're sleeping on the porch."

"Yes, Lady. Your wish is my command…"

I practically ran into my room and dove under the covers. Only when I had shut the light off and nestled my head in the pillows, did the smile find its way to my face.

∞ ∞ ∞

The smell of *fresh* coffee woke me up. Not surprising since Jimmy was holding a steaming mug inches from my face and wafting the steam toward me. I blinked and groaned.

"What time is it?"

"After ten. Josie left, said something about hanging out with someone or other. Chief called your phone no less than three times. Oh, and your mother hasn't *stopped* calling. I didn't answer."

"I left my phone in the kitchen?"

"Yes."

"Is that coffee for me?"

"Yes."

"I'm keeping you."

"That was my plan."

I chuckled and sat up, taking the mug from him and tasting it. He made even better coffee than me. I seriously debated chaining him in the basement. I blushed as that thought led to other thoughts. Happy little thoughts.

"Thanks for the coffee."

"Thanks for the wonderful morning view."

I looked down. The comforter had slipped down exposing my bare breasts. "You're welcome."

With a confidence I didn't feel, I peeled the cover off and strode to the bathroom, shutting the door behind me. I didn't mind if he saw me naked, but I'd be damned if I peed in front of him.

I brushed my teeth and by the time I got out of the bathroom, he was sitting patiently in the kitchen. "Morning," I said formally.

"Morning, Lady."

"Save it for the Coven."

"Still not comfortable?"

"That day *may* come, but today is not that day."

"I hear you. Not one for ceremony myself."

"You're an interesting fella, Jimmy. And why Jimmy instead of James or Jim?"

"It's what they called me in school, many, many years ago. Dennis read it in my old yearbook and told the guys at the station. It kind of stuck."

125

"Ah. Well what do you prefer? I'll call you something else if you want."

"Nah. Whole town picked up on it. I don't mind it. What about you? Why Dot?"

"Because Dorothea makes me sound like a pretentious puritanical prick."

"I can see that. Why not Dorothy?"

"Seriously? Can you just imagine all the Kansas jokes when technically they should be making jokes about dropping houses on *me*?"

"I see your point."

"Yeah." I looked down at my phone. Twenty-three missed calls and only three from Chief.

"I guess I should call my mother."

"Yeah. I need to get home. Thanks for everything."

I narrowed my eyes and pointed at him.

"I was referring to the use of your couch and your coffee. Nothing more." He held up his hands defensively.

"Okay. I'll let you live."

"Bless you, Lady." He gave me a wink. "So, this is the awkward part. Hug? Kiss? Or should I just run while I'm ahead."

I tipped my head to the side, thinking for a moment. "Hug definitely. Maybe a quick peck on the lips. No tongue though. Way too early for that."

He walked around the counter and wrapped me in his arms. I'll admit, it felt good. Especially when he sensuously brushed his lips across mine and then kissed me gently.

"Bye, Dot. Have a good day."

"You, too. Stay safe."

"I will try."

He left quietly through the front door as I stared at its white paint. Jimmy was defnititely...*interesting*. I'd fooled around with more than a few guys, but nothing recent. In my entire ninety-nine years of life, I'd had exactly one boyfriend. He'd packed up and moved to Europe with his mother. I'd been devastated. He was the reason for my hiatus from dating. Jimmy, on the other hand, I could see sticking around for quite a while. While I wasn't exactly ready to call him my boyfriend, yet, I didn't find the idea unappealing in any way.

In fact, judging by the smile on my face, I liked the idea. I thought about him a little more and felt the fluttering in my chest. The more I thought about him, the steadier it became and the happier I felt.

Oh, shit. I really like him.

Sighing, I picked up my phone and decided to call Chief first to try and get my mind off Jimmy. He picked up on the third ring.

"Morning, sunshine."

"Morning, Chief. Sorry I missed your call. Late night."

"No worries. I was going to interview some of the Coven this afternoon. Would you mind tagging along?"

"Not at all. I offered."

"Wanna have lunch with me first?"

"Sure. Diner?"

"Sounds good. See you there, unless you want a ride?"

"I'll meet you there."

"Thanks, Dot. I mean that."

The line clicked dead.

I could almost hear ominous music playing in the background as I dialed my mother.

∞ ∞ ∞

"Hi, Marge."

"Hey, sweetie. Grab your table. I'll be right there."

I sat down in the booth and watched the people passing by the window. Main Street looked a little livelier than it had the past week.

"What you want to drink?"

"Coke. What's going on outside?"

"They're starting to put up the Christmas decorations."

"And that draws a crowd?"

"Townful of busybodies. Won't see me out there gawkin'."

"Seems like they put them up earlier and earlier every year. Back home is the same way. Halloween over, *boom* let's put up the Christmas shit."

"Think they do that to get people to spend money, Dot."

"Yep."

"Know what you want to eat or get your Coke first?"

"Waiting on Chief, but I'll have the patty melt with fries."

"I'll start the orders. I know what he wants."

"He call it in?"

"No, sweetie. He's been eating the same damn thing for ten years."

"I can truly picture that."

"Be right back."

As soon as she slid behind the counter, Chief walked in. He smiled when he saw me. I melted a little on the inside. A little pang of Jimmy guilt hit me right in the chest. I wasn't expecting *that*.

"Hey," he said smoothly and slid into the booth across from me.

"Hey, yourself. I ordered for us. Since you were late."

He glanced down at his watch. "I'm five minutes early."

"Whatever. Ordered you a liverwurst sandwich, dry."

The disgusted look that crossed his face made it totally worth it. "What?"

"Just kidding. Marge said she knows what you want."

"Oh, damn. I was actually going to try something different today."

"Really?"

"No."

"You suck."

"You started it." He grinned. "You seem a little happier today than you have in a while. Have good dreams?"

The color drained from my face. "Yeah. Dreams."

He gave me a puzzled look and shook his head. Thankfully Marge showed up with our drinks. "Foods cookin'. Be out in a minute or two."

"Thanks, Marge." I wanted to hug her.

"So, what happened last night?" He started right back up.

Damn it.

I opened my mouth to tell some elaborate lie, but I stopped myself. The Chief and I weren't dating. I didn't have any reason to lie. "Jimmy stopped by last night, drunk off his ass. I threw him in my shower."

There. The truth.

"And? You're giggling like a school girl this morning because you saw him naked?"

"No. We fooled around."

The truth, and nothing but the truth.

Chief nodded appreciatively. "Cool."

Cool? So, help me, Lady.

I almost let out a little gasp when disappointment settled in my stomach. Maybe Chief wasn't actually interested in me. He was hard to read, but I thought the signs were there. Not that I was an expert in the field or anything. I tried to shove the disappointment away. Jimmy was definitely interested and that was more than enough.

But, damnit. Chief is sexy as hell, too.

"When was the um… Never mind. Insensitive question." I should have known better than to ask.

"When was the last time I fooled around?"

I nodded.

"Two years."

"Sorry, Chief. I should have known."

He shrugged. He'd taken it better than I expected. Or deserved. I felt guilty.

"Jimmy's good people. Dennis, too."

"You say that like they're a package deal."

"They kind of are," he said with a chuckle. "Work together, two jobs, live together. See one, the other's usually right behind him."

That got the brain cells firing. "They aren't um…"

"Gay? Nah. Just good friends."

"Gotcha. Is anybody in the coven gay? Not that it matters. Just curious. Josie is bi."

"Candace."

"The tiny blonde?"

He nodded.

"Hmm. Josie went somewhere with someone today. Wonder if it was her. She swore off men for a while after Richie's…death."

"Well, good luck to her. Candace is a little…strange."

"Because she's gay?"

"Hell no. Because she talks to rocks and animals."

"Oh."

"Fae is the word I'd use."

"She does have pointed ears."

"She's sweet. Just weird."

It was time to change the subject. "Who are we interviewing first?"

"Jason."

I sighed.

"Don't like him?"

"He didn't give me a reason to." I took a sip of my coke.

"Don't judge him before you get to know him. He has reason to be a little standoffish."

"What reason could that possibly be?"

"He's my brother-in-law."

Oh. Shit. Smooth, Dot.

"Okay. I'll cut him lots of slack. Strange lady coming in and changing everything. I get it." I felt like a dick.

"You didn't know. No worries. But that *is* the reason he was upset about the coven name changing."

"I don't blame him. I wasn't expecting that either. Lady only knows why she did it."

"That was amazing by the way."

"Don't go there. I'm still freaked out about it. Stepping out of your body isn't something I ever want to do again. Ever."

"We could still see you. You were just kind of see through and glowy."

"Glowy. Pretty sure that's not a word."

"Well, I would have said glowing, but I already used that word to describe you this morning…"

"Oh, my God. You suck."

"Do you?"

I stared at him incredulously as he started laughing. "I can't believe you just said that. Do the men in my life take great *pleasure* in watching me blush?"

"I don't know about the rest, but I do."

I shook my head and sipped my coke. I was literally speechless. Chief was still laughing when Marge brought our food.

"He okay?" She asked me but pointed at him.

"For now. I may kill him after our meal, though."

"Herb, you're gonna have another customer," she shouted to the kitchen.

Apparently, I couldn't say anything right.

JACQUELYN FAYE

Chapter 14

"Dot, I swear I was just teasing. I didn't mean to make you uncomfortable."

"Yeah, yeah. Drop it."

"Are you mad at me?"

"No," I lied and enjoyed the scenery. Jason didn't live *in* town. He lived twenty minutes outside of town up a dirt road and over a couple of hills. Chief offered to drive so I didn't waste my gas. I considered it to avoid being in the same vehicle.

"You know I consider you a friend. This is the sort of witty banter that friends have. That should make you happy."

"I'm honored."

"You don't sound it." He chuckled again.

"Honestly, I'm happy. You consider us friends. It's just last night was unlike me. It started out innocently enough. At least we didn't fuck."

"Gonna let you in on a little secret. It wouldn't have been the end of the world if you had. You would still be you this morning. No shame in having a good time. You're both single."

"True," I said feeling a little better. "Thanks."

He patted my leg.

It sent a shiver up my spine.

I was still horny.

What the hell? Must be all the fresh air.

He pulled up to a trailer in the middle of the woods. Literally. It was surrounded by trees except for the front. A

133

beat up nineteen-sixty-something Buick was parked in front. I thought it was painted brown, but it was literally covered in rust. I needed a tetanus shot just looking at it.

"Think he would like me more if I bought him a car?"

"Don't make fun of Bessie. That would piss him off more than anything."

"Yeah. I have that effect on people."

"You're not wrong there."

"Shut up. You find me charming."

"Sure. Let's go with that…"

I tried to look indignant as he parked next to the rust monster. I must have failed immensely. He ignored me, so I pouted. "Meanie."

"Chief Meanie to you."

"I'm putting the Dick back in your title."

"You should probably stay away from dick for a few days…"

I almost started crying. "Wow…"

"It was a joke! Don't take it so hard. Oh, wow. Even that came out wrong…"

My tears turned into fits of giggles.

"You're very frustrating. You know that?"

I nodded. "Yep. I've been told that before."

Chief patted my head. "You'll grow out of it one day."

"Nope. I refuse. It's one of my most endearing qualities."

He rolled his eyes and opened the car door. I got out and followed him up the wooden step to the front door. He knocked loudly. "Jason. It's me."

There was a loud *thump* and what sounded like the tinkling of beer bottles being kicked. The door opened, and a haggard looking Jason pressed his face against the screen door.

"Bill?"

"Yeah. Have to ask you a few questions."

"About what?" He opened the door and let him in, then he noticed me standing behind him.

"Mornin', Jason."

"Lady." His voice sounded distant and cool. It was better than close and angry. My day was looking up.

He let me through and let go of the screen door. It slammed shut and he shut the weather door. It was almost balmy inside the trailer. And smelled like he hadn't thrown anything out in a couple of weeks. Maybe months. I fought the urge to gag.

"Lady bright. You need to clean up in here, dude," Chief chided him.

"It's the cleaning lady's week off," he replied, unimpressed.

He led us to the small living room, the tube TV playing some football game with the sound off. He picked up his beer and motioned to the couch next to his big recliner.

I warily sat, pushing a half-empty bag of Doritos and a sandwich crust out of the way. I refrained from speaking. I didn't want him to hear the disgust in my voice. Josie was a slob. This guy was beyond that by several orders of magnitude.

"So, what's up?"

"Another murder."

"Besides Richie?"

Chief nodded. "Dane."

"No fucking way!"

I could tell he was visibly upset by the news. Dane was friends with Chief, Chief was Jason's brother-in-law. It made sense. I could tell just from his reaction we were barking up the wrong tree. But then again, I wasn't a cop.

"I guess your shield plan failed," he shot angrily at me.

I shrugged and held up my hands. "He wasn't burned to death. Whoever did it tried. Then they slashed his throat."

Jason blinked in surprise. "We're tough, but not having your throat slashed tough. Spelled and slashed. At least we can rule out the mortals. That just leaves the coven..."

"Why we're here. Where were you last night?"

"Working. You can check with the foreman at the plant."

"I figured as much, just had to ask."

"I know the drill."

Chief nodded and looked at me. "You have any questions for him?"

"No. I didn't think he did it the moment you told him what happened."

Chief stood, and I did the same.

"Dwight was working with me last night. You can rule him out. I'll save you the trip."

"Thanks. That helps. That guy lives in BFE."

"Worse than this?"

"This is the suburbs. Dwight lives off grid. He's a survivalist. No power, nothing. You need four-wheel drive just to get to his trailer."

"That's kind of scary."

"Not if you like your privacy," Jason answered.

"Is that why you live out here?"

"I thought you didn't have any further questions."

I shrugged. "Just curious. I like to know the people in our coven."

"It's not really our coven any more. It's yours."

"Jason," Chief warned.

I held up my hand. "Give us a minute, Chief?"

"You sure?"

"I'm sure."

"I'll be in the car."

I watched him leave the way we came in. It was time for a little tough love. During our conversation, I'd noticed one small detail. Jason didn't have his shield up.

"*Ná bogadh.*" I didn't use the Chief's binding spell. I simply uttered the words to immobilize the angry man.

"What did you do?"

"Made it so you couldn't move. You see, Jason," I sat down on his lap and stared directly into his eyes, "I noticed that you didn't have your shields up. If I were a murderer, I could have turned you into a charcoal briquette by now. Do you see why I *begged* all of you to use them. To be safe?"

"Yes. Let me go."

"In a minute. You and I are going to have a much needed talk first."

"Let me go and we can talk."

"No. You might not listen. This way I can drive my point *home*." I poked him in the chest as I emphasized the word.

"First of all, this is not my coven. It is *our* coven. I understand that you might think I'm trying to make it mine since your sister is gone, but that is not the case. Everything shall be put to vote in regards to governing the coven. I'm no dictator. I didn't even want to be high priestess. I'm just trying to give you guys a chance at being whole again."

He blinked in surprise. "Okay."

"You have been confrontational since the moment you laid eyes on me. I have done *nothing* to deserve that. I'm not asking you to like me, Jason. I'm just asking you to give me a chance. Okay?"

He sighed in defeat. I stood up and pulled the magic off him, letting him move again. I offered him my hand, and surprisingly enough, he took it.

"I'm sorry, Lady."

"Just call me Dot."

"Okay."

"Jason?"

"Yes?"

"Seriously. Clean this place up, though. It's disgusting. I feel like chugging penicillin just from sitting on your couch."

He laughed for the first time since I'd met him. It was a beautiful laugh and his smile could light up any room. He needed to do both more. "Yes, ma'am."

"Are you doing okay?" I sat back down. "I know losing your sister must have been hard, and I'm not trying to be your therapist, just concerned."

He kept standing and crossed his arms, toeing one of the many beer bottles on the floor. "Yeah. I'm doin' okay."

Sounded like bullshit to me.

"Can I be honest?"

"I'd prefer it if you weren't."

"Yeah. Not my strong suit. You don't look like you're doing okay. Do you do anything besides work at the factory?"

"Not much else to do but drink."

"Life is what you make of it, not what it makes of you. Would you like some company every once in a while? I'm sure being out here in the boonies by yourself isn't helping."

"You asking me out on a date?" He seemed incredulous.

"No. But if you'd like to, I would. You working tomorrow night?"

"No. I'm actually off for two days."

"Good. Come to my house for dinner."

"Seriously?"

"Very."

"Okay. I will."

I gave him a small smile and stood back up. "Well, I should get going. Chief probably thinks I'm in here beating you senseless."

"I thought that's what you were going to do there for a minute…"

"I almost did. If there's any food stuck to the back of my jeans, I still might." I wiped my butt off with my hands. I didn't feel anything. "Nope. You're good." I winked and headed for the door.

His tentative hand on my arm stopped me. "Thanks. Sorry if I came off as an asshole."

"I'm sorry if I did."

He shook his head. "No. You've been nice since the moment I met you. Just didn't know how to deal with the situation. Even when I wasn't being nice, you were never rude. You're just kind of scary."

"Everybody keeps telling me that. I think it might be the red hair."

"I think it's more than that. Your eyes. Your determined look. Your overwhelming presence. You're like a hurricane in a small woman's body."

"That might be the nicest thing anybody has ever said to me." I teared up a little. "Thanks, Jason." I scooted closer to him and gave him a quick hug. "See you tomorrow."

"See you tomorrow, Dot."

I exited the trailer and got back into Chief's car. He had the heat going and was listening to country music. He laughed when he saw my face. "Not a fan?"

"Of people whining about their trucks, girlfriends, and horses? Hell no."

"I'll change the station."

"Then I won't jump out of the car when you're going sixty."

"Maybe I'll leave it on then."

"Why are you so mean to me?"

"Cuz you're so damn perfect it annoys me."

"Oh, really?"

He put it in reverse and backed away from the trailer. I slipped back into my seat as he gunned it, spraying dirt behind us and fishtailing the Jeep.

"Having fun?"

He nodded.

"How am I too perfect? I get under your skin. I tease you at every opportunity. I'm a constant thorn in your side."

"As you said. Those are some of your most endearing qualities."

"You're a strange man."

"That's one of *my* most endearing qualities. How did it go with Jason? You didn't hurt him, did you?"

"Nope. He apologized, and we have a date tomorrow."

"A what?"

"Date. It's when a guy and a girl do something fun together."

"With Jason?" I couldn't help but notice the awe in his voice.

"Yes. With Jason."

"You're good."

"At what?"

"I haven't figured that out yet, but I'll let you know."

"Why, Chief. Are you jealous?"

"Of?"

"Me on a date with your brother-in-law."

I expected him to vehemently deny it. I wasn't expecting him to say, "Yes. A little."

Chapter 15

"What?"

"You heard me."

"I didn't think you were ready to date again."

"I'm probably not."

"Now I'm confused."

"So am I." He sighed and looked out the window at the trees passing us by.

"You're not ready to date, but you want to date?"

"Not quite. I want to date you."

"Chief... I'm already seeing Jimmy. Now I have a date with Jason. Though that's more of me wanting to get him out of that disgusting trailer and have a little fun, but still. Why?"

"Don't worry about it."

"Not going to happen. Talk to me."

"You're beautiful. You're charming. Sometimes. You make me laugh, you make me want to punch things. You're frustrating and scary and you amaze me."

What the fuck?

"Okay."

"Okay, what?"

"Let's go out. For dinner. You're buying."

"Where?"

"I'll leave that up to you. This town has to have a restaurant a *little* fancier than the diner."

"There's a couple."

"Pick one. And pick me up Friday night."

"Yes, ma'am."

"Don't call me that. Jason did and now I'm finding it a little creepy. Wait. You're not going to ask me to break my date with him, are you?"

"No way in hell. I'm not a possessive freak. You asked him out first. This is a date, not a relationship. Yet," he added with a wink.

I leaned back into my seat, a little excited at the prospect. "Where we heading next?"

"That's it for now. I couldn't get ahold of anyone but Jason. I was hoping to catch Dwight at his compound, but he has an ailibi."

"Sounds good to me. That was almost exhausting. Don't know how you do this police stuff all the time."

"Sarcasm. Another endearing quality."

"That sounded like sarcasm."

"Maybe." The corner of his mouth turned upward in the beginning of a smile.

He parked in front of the diner and left the engine running.

"Thanks for the ride."

"Thanks for coming with me."

I opened my door and slid out of the Jeep, dropping to the ground. Jeeps, even Cherokees, were not made for smaller people. I was taller than average and still had a difficult time. Getting in was worse.

"Let me know when you need me next," I said and reached to close the door.

"I'll refrain from making a dirty comment…"

I sighed and shut the door. He might be hot, but he was frustrating as fuck. I waved as he pulled away. When he turned into to the station, I got into my car and started her up, cranking the heat.

I felt the spell trigger. Focusing my energy into my shield, I screamed, "*Sciath cloiche*!"

My shield coalesced and hardened to stone as the dashboard of my Kia exploded inward as the engine blew up in a gigantic fireball, shooting my hood straight up into the air. Even through the shield I felt the impact of force and it doubled as the gas tank behind me caught and went. The ringing in my ears almost drove me insane, but it was the heat that sucked the air from my lungs and plunged me into darkness.

∞ ∞ ∞

Beep. Beep. Beep.

It was the only sound that greeted me when I came to.

I was lying in a bed, or assumed I was. It felt like a bed, though I couldn't open my eyes to verify. I reached out and felt metal rails on either side. A stinging sensation in my forearm caught my attention. Even unable to see, I knew it was an IV needle.

Hospital. I'm in a hospital. I'm alive. Sweet Lady, I'm alive. I wonder how bad the damage is...

I opened my mouth and tried to call out. I managed a weak cough. It felt like the inside of my lungs were coated in soot. I reached up and felt the oxygen tube in my nose. I counted my blessings there wasn't a tube in my throat. I probably would have puked waking up to that.

"You're awake?"

Recognizing Chief's voice, I nodded.

"Nurse!"

His chair slid backward, and I felt his hands gently grab mine.

"Yes?"

"She's awake."

"I'll be damned. She is one tough cookie."

"You have no idea."

"Can you hear me, sweetie?"

I nodded again. Not even wanting to try and speak.

"You've been in an accident."

I tilted my head and gave her a dirty look. I hope she could tell it was dirty with a swollen face and closed eyes.

It didn't go unnoticed. "Your eyelids are swollen shut, but the doctor doesn't think there is any damage. You did inhale a good amount of smoke, but again, there doesn't seem to be any permanent damage. Other than a nasty bump to your head, you came out relatively unscathed. Even your hair didn't get singed. The angels were with you today, young lady."

Oh, thank the Lady. Blessed be.

I wanted to cry, but my eyelids didn't even let me do that. If I could speak, I might be able to heal myself a little. It wasn't one of my major talents, but anything to help would be great.

"Are you thirsty?"

My throat feels like an ashtray. Of course, I'm thirsty. I nodded emphatically at her.

I felt the straw touch my lips and took a tentative sip. I could feel it soothing my cracked and parched throat as it slid down. I even pictured little wisps of steam when she pulled the straw away.

"Better?"

"Yes," I managed to croak. I sounded like a muppet gargling broken glass.

"Okay. Relax for a while. The doctor should be in to check on you shortly."

I nodded and melted into my pillow, listening to her squeaky footsteps as she left the room.

"What happened?" Chief whispered after she left.

"My car exploded." I choked out.

"Yeah. I kind of knew that much. I pulled you out of the burning rubble."

"Thanks."

"I'm guessing it wasn't an accident?"

144

I shook my head. "Felt the spell. Turned on the heater and kaboom."

"How the hell did you manage to survive?"

"Stoneshield. Talk later?"

"Sorry. Yes."

He surprised me when he bent over and kissed me on the forehead. I smiled, or at least I hoped I did, up at him. Hopefully, I didn't look like a deranged ash-monster doing it.

"Thank you," he whispered.

"What?"

"For not dying."

"My pleasure."

"I'll be back to check on you in a while. One of the other officers will be guarding your door. He has a list of people who can see you. I put Josie on it. I texted her from your phone since I don't have her number. She should be here any time."

I nodded my gratefulness.

"I have a street to go clean up. By the way, you're going to need a new car. Call your insurance when you can. There isn't enough for them to do much of an investigation, though."

I nodded, only slightly caring. I did love my Soul, but it was just a car at the end of the day.

"I'll see you in a little while."

I waved at him, wanting nothing more than a little silence.

It lasted all of five minutes.

I heard the whirlwind that was my best friend outside the door. She was arguing about something with the police officer. I smiled. A little normalcy might be nice. She finally made it past him and entered the room.

"Oh, my Lady. Are you okay?"

I couldn't see her, but I could hear the pain in her voice. "Yeah. They tell me I'm fine. My head hurts and I can't see, but I'll be fine in a while. Once the swelling goes down."

"Someone did this to you?"

"My car. It sploded."

"I know that! It's the only damn thing the whole town is talking about. I heard about it from Marge before Chief texted."

She was pouting. I could hear it in her voice. "Sorry. I was unconscious. Blown up, sir."

"I can't believe you're okay. You're really okay, right? Not faking it?"

"I'm fine. I got my stone shield up in time. Just the impact hurt my face. My eyes are swollen."

I felt her cool hand touch my face. She whispered, "*Sana cito*." A cold tingling sensation spread through my forehead and face. Literally, I could feel the swelling going down. I still couldn't open my eyes, but I wasn't nearly as uncomfortable.

"Thanks."

"Sorry I couldn't help more."

"You're better at healing than I am."

"Yeah. Well, you're better at everything else. So, let me have this one."

"Fine. You're coven healer."

"Isn't that what gamer guys make their girlfriends? Does this mean we're dating now?"

"Please. Besides. I heard you got yourself a girlfriend already."

"Not yet. But I'm working on it. She is adorable."

"Just be careful."

"Cough–Jimmy–Cough."

"Shut up."

"Grumpy."

"Help me up, would you? I got to pee."

"Let me get the nurse. You still have the IV and are tied to all kinds of machines."

"Is the IV on a rolly cart?"

"Yeah?"

146

I slid off the bed and ripped the monitoring clamp off my index finger, ignoring the blaring alarm. "I *really* have to pee. Help me to the bathroom."

"You are so stubborn."

"Yes. She is. There's a bedpan right next to the bed." The irate sounding nurse was tapping her foot from the doorway.

"Well, my friend didn't tell me *that*. Since I'm up, may I please use the bathroom?"

"Yes, but let me help you over there. Hospital liability issue."

I held out my arm. She slipped under it. I took a tentative step forward, grateful for her assistance. I was a little wobblier than I was expecting.

"Your balance is probably off because of the whack you took to the head. Not being able to see isn't helping."

"It will come back, right?"

"Doc took X-rays. Said there was no damage. I'm sure you'll be fine. Most people who blow up, actually blow up. Care to share how you're still in once piece and not all over Main Street?"

"Kia has the highest safety ratings for small to mid-sized sedans *and* SUVs."

"You're a strange lady."

"It's one of my most endearing qualities. Or so people keep telling me."

She got me down on the seat and thanks to the wonders of modern hospital gowns, I didn't have to do anything.

"Ahh. Thanks."

"Sir, you're going to have to wait outside for a moment."

I shook my head. "Which one is it?"

"It's me." Jimmy's voice threatened to crack with laughter.

"It's okay, nurse. He's seen me naked."

"I bet he has. You seen him? Got any pictures?"

I started laughing. At least I got the cool nurse. I finished up and the nurse helped me back into bed, draping the blanket over my legs.

"Let me go find the doc, tell him you're up and about. I'll be back."

"Thanks."

"Heard you had a rough afternoon." He'd tried for lighthearted and witty, but sounded more worried and afraid.

"You have no idea. Somebody blew up my car with me in it."

"Look at the bright side. You're still here."

"Yeah. Goody. My head wishes I weren't."

"It doesn't look bad at all. Looks like your forehead swelled and drained into your eyes. You have some bruising. You won't need eyeshadow for a while."

"Cut me, Mick…"

"That's pretty funny. Now get some rest. You need anything?"

"Just some sleep. And my own bed."

"I don't think they'll let me bring that in here, and I don't think you're going home tonight."

"I figured."

"Want some company?"

"No, not really right now, at least I have a cop guarding the door so I don't have to worry about them trying again. I'm in a shitty mood anyway. You working tomorrow?"

"No."

Trepidation filled me, and a little fear. I wanted to be honest with Jimmy, but I was unsure on how he was going to respond. "I'm going to be honest with you. I have a date tomorrow with Jason. I invited him over to get him out of that trailer."

"I know. And you're going out with Bill on Friday."

"Seriously, how the fuck do you people keep doing shit like this? Did you plant a microphone on me?" I wanted more than anything to see his face, to judge his reaction.

He laughed. "No. I saw him in the lobby."

"And you guys just happened to discuss my dating schedule?"

"Amongst other things."

"*What*?"

"Kidding."

"Then how did you know?"

"Oh, not about that part. He really did tell me, so I didn't make plans and then you have to break them."

"You don't mind?"

He leaned over and kissed me on the forehead. "You are the head of our coven. You can date whomever you want. Even if you weren't, I just met you a week ago. I wouldn't presume…"

"I've stepped into the Twilight Zone. That's the only explanation."

"No. Welcome to Cedar Falls."

"Did Bill's wife…?"

"No! They were married before she became high priestess. Besides, those two were so in love you couldn't stick a fork between them."

"Gotcha."

"Alright. I'm gonna go home. Call me if you need anything."

"I will. Thanks, Jimmy."

"No problem."

I let the trepidation and fear go. If neither of them had a problem with me dating more than one of them, I wasn't going to look a gift horse in the mouth. I'd worry about it *when* it became a problem. I just wondered how long I had…

Chapter 16

The mid-morning sun glaring off the new snow outside the hospital threatened to drive me back inside. My eyes had stopped being swollen in the middle of the night, and I could see again. But damn I was snow-blind.

"You okay?"

I nodded at Chief. "Bright."

"Here." He took his sunglasses off and put them on my eyes.

"Bless you. And thanks for picking me up."

"Well, it's not like you had a ride home."

He opened the door and helped me into the Jeep. I missed my Kia already. "Thanks."

He practically ran around the other side of the car. "I also took the liberty of calling your insurance. They weren't too happy, but sent an adjuster out this morning from Syracuse. I let him inspect the wreckage."

"Thanks. That's something off my plate."

"Yeah."

"What's up? You're acting weird."

"What do you mean?" He coughed nervously.

"Chief William Bob Jingleheimershmidt, or whatever your name was… What did you do?"

We pulled onto my street. Luckily, I wasn't far from the hospital. Just out of decrepit walking distance. I looked at the house and on my front stoop. For a brief moment, I thought Josie was waiting outside for me. She wasn't, but my *mother* was…

"Oh, no you fucking didn't."

"Surprise," he said weakly.

I literally thought about incinerating him on the spot. If he wasn't driving, I might have. "We will discuss this later," I said through my clenched teeth, plastering a fake smile on my lips and waving to my mother.

"I thought I was doing good," he whispered back. "Then I met her."

"That isn't punishment enough."

"Sorry."

Without another word, I opened my own damn door and slid out of the SUV myself, wincing in a little pain as I landed.

"Are you okay, sweetie?" She rushed over and helped me steady myself.

"Hi, Mother."

"Don't you dare 'Hi, Mother me. You don't tell me where you are, you don't answer my calls. Then you go and get yourself blown up! What the hell, Dorothea?"

"Mother. My head hurts. Can we discuss this inside, out of view of the rest of the county?"

"Don't get smart with me, young lady."

"Inside. Go. Shoo."

She growled and stomped her foot as only my mother could, but she did walk up the stairs and into the house. That's when I noticed Josie staring at me hopelessly out her front window. I waved at her and rolled my eyes.

"I thought *you* were scary. Is your mother really a witch?"

"What else would she be?"

"I don't know. Italian? Demon?"

I sighed. He wasn't far from the truth. I wondered myself sometimes. "No. Holy water works on both of those. I tried it."

He chuckled.

"No!" I rounded on him, my finger shaking in his face. "You don't get to laugh. You're in deep shit. This is your doing! You better take me to the nicest restaurant in Syracuse for this one. Only through pain will you learn that the demon mother must *never* be called."

He laughed even harder.

"You owe me dessert now, too."

He pressed his lips against mine. Magically, it shut me up.

"What are you doing?"

"Kissing you?"

"Why?"

"Seemed like a plausible way to get you to stop yelling at me."

"Shut up and kiss me again."

He did. The scratchiness of his unshaven face was quite the contrast to Jimmy's almost boyish skin. He tasted like coffee and heat. I felt myself getting dizzy and it didn't have anything to do with trauma to my inner ear...

He pulled back and looked me in the eye. "Better?"

"Yes. But I might need more therapy after dealing with my mother. You better take responsibility."

"Oh, I will. Are you still up for dinner with Jason tonight?"

"Shit."

"I told him what happened. He was worried about you, but not you missing the date. Want me to tell him to come or postpone?

"He's off tomorrow isn't he?"

"Yes."

"Tell him I'm taking him to dinner. There's no way I'm going to subject that poor boy to meeting my mother on the first date."

"I'll let him know."

"Thanks, Chief. You coming in?"

"Uh. No. I have some…um…paperwork back at the office. I just snuck away to bring you home."

"You are a horrible liar."

"Yes," he said and kissed me one more time, a soft brush of a kiss. "Good luck."

He turned around and got back in his Jeep. He didn't even help me up the stairs. "Thanks, Dick!"

He waved and backed out of the driveway. I'd take it out of his hide later. I turned around and walked to the steps, hanging on to the iron railing with everything I had. It wasn't really to steady me. I was more slowing my ascent into the pit of hell that waited for me through the front door.

Josie came out and helped me.

"Has it been bad?"

"Nuclear biohazard zombie apocalypse bad."

"Sorry. Chief thought he was being helpful."

"Oh, I already ripped him a new one." She chuckled evilly.

"Look at the bright side. Your mother didn't come."

"Wrong! But thank you for playing. She is currently at the motel in the room adjacent to your mother's. I have been berated and humiliated all morning."

"Oh, shit."

"Yeah. Best day *ever*."

"So, what am I walking into?'

"You got blowed up. What you think gonna happen?'

I sighed and opened the front door, resigned to my fate…

Mother sat coolly on my sofa, sipping tea and staring off into space. She didn't acknowledge my entrance or existence, just continued sipping and sipping some more.

Great. She's gathering her thoughts.

"Do you hate me?" She began, and I groaned.

I plopped down on the love seat. Josie made a mad dash back to Josie-land. *Coward!*

"No, Mother. I don't hate you. I'm sorry for not calling you, but this move was to start my own life. How can I do that if I don't do it by myself?"

She didn't hesitate. "A visitation from the Lady herself? I'm sorry, Dorothea, but *that* deserved a phone call. Getting yourself blown up? Phone call. Murders? Guess what? Phone call!"

"Sorry," I said meekly. She kind of *did* have a point. Small one.

"What am I going to with you?"

"I'm not going back home, Mother!"

She held up her hand. "No. You are not. If you were not smack dab in the middle of exactly where you were supposed to be, the Lady would not have shown you her favor. I am not here to bring you home. Nor am I here to guide you. I just missed you and wanted to make sure you were really all right."

By the time she finished her lengthy sentence, her voice cracked a little and I noticed that which might have been the very beginnings of a tear. A lump formed in my throat.

I moved from my seat to the open spot on the sofa next to her, leaning against her. "Did you have to bring Miranda? Josie's a hot mess now."

Mother chuckled. "She knows all about your tales. She is as equally as impressed as I am. She was a little stricter with her rules than I, though. Count your blessings, daughter."

"Always. You can be scary and a pain in the ass, but I do love you. Most of the time."

"And where do you think you got your charm from?"

"Dad?"

She swatted me on the top of my head. I winced in pain and let out a little *yelp*.

"Oh, Dot. I'm sorry! I forgot."

"It was worth it!" I looked up at her and smiled.

"What?"

"You called me Dot."

∞ ∞ ∞

"Welcome to the Cedar Falls diner, Mother."

"It's very greenish-blue."

"Teal. Don't let the décor fool you, the food is superb."

My mother was many things. High priestess. Haughty. Snobbish. Overbearing. The list goes on and on. But, one thing she truly excelled at, was appreciating food. I grew up eating out. It was safer for everybody than letting my mother into a kitchen. If it didn't involve a cauldron, she was lost. Over the years we rotated through *every* restaurant in Ashville, several hundred times. There are a lot of meals in ninety-nine years...

Her favorite and mine had to be the classic diner. There was just something about the food. It didn't matter the meal or the time of day. You could order an omelet for dinner or a burger for breakfast. The food just warmed you up. She was even a huge fan of Guy Fieri.

"Hi, hon. How you feeling?"

"Hey, Marge. This is my mother, Madeline."

"Oh! Pleased to meet you. You have a wonderful daughter."

"I know." She began to peruse the menu.

I rolled my eyes at Marge.

"Coke?"

"Please."

"And what would you like to drink, Mrs. Blackwell?"

"I would love a cup of coffee and a large orange juice."

"Be right back with those." Marge headed off.

"Mother. Please be nice. I know you can. You do it at home."

"To those humans whom I've interacted with for years, dear. I'm not going to be nice to someone I just met. It just isn't done."

"Believe it or not. You're not wrong there. But try for my sake. Please."

"Very well."

"Here you are, ladies." Marge set our drinks down on the table.

"Thanks, Marge."

"Know what you want to eat?"

"I'll have the turkey platter."

"Steak omelet, please."

"Sounds good. Have it right out."

"The coffee is delicious," Mother said after Marge had left.

"The cook is also the real estate agent, title company, and coroner."

She slowly set her coffee back down, staring at it.

"The food is safe mother. He wears gloves."

"I despise real estate agents. You know that."

"Okay. Not where I thought you were going with that. Anyhoo, the town is hurting. People are doing what they can to keep it alive."

"Yes. Josie told me about your book store."

"Shit!"

"Dorothea, language."

"I was supposed to hear from the contractor yesterday."

"Call him back. I'm sure he'll understand you exploding."

"True. He probably already knows. News travels faster here than in Ashville. By the way. You need to have our police records destroyed. Luckily the Chief here is part of the coven, but anybody can see those records."

"I'll have a chat with Chief Winslow when I get back."

"Thank you. What happened with the mayor?"

"I removed the hex, but not before the townsfolk started referring to him as Mayor Shithead. It worked out beautifully."

"You're pure evil."

157

"Not pure, dear. By any stretch of the imagination."

"More than I needed to know."

"So, I hear you are quite popular with the male townsfolk."

"We are not having this conversation."

"You had a gentleman caller the night before? And you cancelled your evening plans tonight?"

I was going to kill Josie.

"And a date with the Chief on Friday, Mother. Let it go, please."

"Oh. I did not hear about that one."

I groaned.

We were saved from further discussion with a well-timed delivery of turkey and omelet. I ignored anything else she might have said and enjoyed my meal. From the looks of it, Mother was enjoying hers as well.

"You were quite right about the place, daughter."

"I know! I love their food."

"What are your plans for the rest of the evening?"

"I thought we might spend some time together."

"I need to get back home. I was thinking of leaving now."

That kind of shocked me. "Are you sure?"

"Yes. You are quite well. It was silly of me to come, but I had to make sure for myself."

"Thanks."

She nodded and actually smiled. "You are doing well here. But be a little more careful in the future. Whomever tried to kill you will certainly try again. And the easiest way to catch them is a well-placed trap. Or figure out what the other victims had in common."

"That's actually somewhat brilliant. I hadn't thought of the trap. As for a commonality between the others, only the killer knows."

"In a town this size? I'm sure there are others *outside* the coven who might have seen something. Perhaps you are barking up the wrong tree?"

My jaw dropped open.

My mother *was* scary.

Scary smart.

"That is brilliant."

"I know," she said with a grin. "Good luck with everything. I shall collect Miranda and be on our way. Thank you for dinner."

"Thank you for coming and your wonderful advice."

"That is always free, my dear. Be safe. Blessed be."

"Blessed be, Mother."

She slipped out of the booth and headed for the door. Marge came over and set the check down on the table. "Is she really your mother?"

"Yes? Why?"

"She looks young enough to be your sister."

"Good genes, Marge. Good genes."

"I want some. Think she'd sell them to me?"

Chapter 17

"Hello?"

Jimmy was kind of cute when he was sleep answering his phone. "Morning, sunshine. You up?"

"In what sense?"

"I'm not asking you if you have morning wood. I'm asking if you're awake."

"What time is it?"

"Eight in the morning."

"No. I'm not up." The line clicked dead.

I called back.

"Dot. Are you on fire right now?"

"No."

"Can you call me back in like two hours?"

"I need you, Jimmy. I need you *real* bad."

"Huh?"

"Yeah. Not having a car sucks. I need you to run me to Syracuse to buy a new one."

"Don't you have to wait for the insurance money?" He groaned.

"Well, I'd get a rental car…you know. If this town had a *rental car place.* So, fuck it. I'm going to buy a new car."

"You can afford to have two car payments until the insurance pays off your other one?"

"I bought that car outright. You get a big discount when you pay with cash."

"I really truly despise you right at this moment."

"But you'll come pick me up?"

He sighed. It was over. I had won. "Yes."

"Okay. I'll buy you breakfast."

"I don't eat breakfast."

"Lunch then."

"Dinner."

"Have plans."

"Didn't say tonight."

"Deal."

"Be there in a bit. Let me at least take a shower." The line clicked dead again.

I left my bedroom and scribbled a note for Josie. She was hanging out with Candace again today, so I wrote good luck and drew a heart on the note. Sometimes I made myself want to throw up.

With a little time to kill, I straightened up the house and put a pot of coffee on. I poured two mugs into travel containers and skipped out the front door. I'd transferred enough money from my primary account over to my local account last night to cover the cost of a new Kia. I didn't have to stop by the bank and pull out cash, but I wanted to. It was worth it to see their faces, and I wasn't kidding. They really do lower the price when you pay in cash. All the dealer fees and games go away.

Jimmy pulled up in his blue pickup. I waved and nearly slipped on some ice on the steps. He was laughing in the truck, I could see him and hear him. I set his mug of coffee down and walked over to the truck, getting in.

"Is that my coffee over there?"

"Yes."

"And you left it over there to punish me for laughing at you?"

"Yes."

"Even though I'm going to drive you an hour to go buy a new car at eight o'clock in the morning on my day off?"

"Yes. After you stop at the bank."

"That's just mean."

"There was ice on the step. I slipped. I could have seriously hurt myself, cracked my skull, and died. You found that funny?"

"A little. Yes. You should have seen your face."

"You're a sick individual, Jimmy."

"Thank you." He didn't argue. He simply got out of the truck, walked over to the stoop, and retrieved his coffee.

"You're welcome," I said as he took his first sip.

"Thank you for the coffee, Lady."

"Thank you for taking me. Seriously though. Could you swing by the bank?"

"Sure."

We pulled out and headed straight there. We had a few minutes to kill as it didn't open until nine. The bank manager recognized me as she was walking by. "Dot?"

"Morning, Mrs. Dolenz."

"Please, call me Jeanne. Come on in."

I followed her in, once she unlocked the door and unset the alarm. She made a face when I told her what I was there for, but told me to wait patiently while they got the vault open.

Fifteen minutes later, Jimmy and I were on our way.

He flipped the radio on as soon as we hit the highway. I braced myself for country, but smiled when I recognized Queen. I started singing along. I wasn't a very good singer, but I didn't care. Cars and showers were made to be sang in.

I glanced over at Jimmy. He looked like he was in pain. I sang louder and started laughing.

"At least you know you suck."

"I do. I recorded myself once," I said, turning down the radio. "I played it back and I couldn't believe what I was hearing. Why do we always sound different in our heads?"

"*Everything* sounds better in our heads."

"Very true. You are a wise man, Jimmy."

"Not all the time."

"See. It takes wisdom to recognize that."

I leaned against the center console separating us in the truck. He took a swig of his coffee and set it down in the holder. Grabbing his hand, I pulled it closer to me, just holding it. I was feeling a little affectionate. I made him miserable this morning, but he came through for me.

"Thanks for taking me. Seriously. Sorry to bother you on your day off, and for being a pain in the ass."

"It's okay. I find it quite endearing and I don't mind helping you out. Ever. Later times would be appreciated, but are not in fact, necessary."

I giggled a little. Instead of holding his hand, I hugged his arm. His hand rested on my thigh. I opened my legs a little and his fingertips slid between them. He wasn't anywhere close to anyplace naughty, and I sighed in disappointment. I was wearing leggings, so it might have been for the best. Walking into the car dealership with a big wet spot on the front of my pants and handing them a wad of cash might get me arrested.

Instead, I just enjoyed his warmth. His heater wasn't the best in the world, so I stole his.

"You smell really good."

I blinked in shock. "Thanks?"

"You do. I don't know what it is either. Smoky but fruity at the same time?"

"The fruit is strawberries from my lotion. The smoky is the perfume I wear. I've worn it for years."

"Sounds like a weird combo, but it works. Really well."

"Does sniffing me turn you on?"

"A little, yes."

I reached over to his lap. Sure enough, he wasn't lying... "Perv."

"You're the one touching Mister Happypants."

I lost it. I started laughing and couldn't stop. "That's better than Captain Nightstick."

"Chief?"

I nodded.

164

"Yeah. Didn't need to know that."

"Sorry."

I leaned over and nibbled on his earlobe, whispering, "Am I forgiven?"

He nodded. "As much as I'm enjoying the attention… We are doing eighty on the highway."

That was all the temptation I needed. I grinned at him evilly and unhooked my seatbelt. "You're right, Jimmy. I shouldn't be distracting you while you're driving." I turned and leaned back against the door, making sure it was locked. I put my feet up on my seat and spread my legs. The silky material of the leggings stretching taught over my mound. I rubbed myself playfully.

"Oh, you suck."

"I do. But I probably shouldn't while you're driving…"

He groaned and squirmed in his seat.

"I could find a rest area or a text stop…"

"Jimmy. I couldn't do anything like that in a public place. I'm way too shy." I pushed myself back in the seat, slipping my leggings down further. "Oops."

I reached down and slid them over my ass and bringing my knees up. Exposing the front of my black lace panties to him.

"Holy fuck," he groaned. He reached down and started rubbing his cock through his jeans.

"Eyes on the road, mister."

I felt the truck jerk as he got fully back in his lane. "Dot. Stop. Seriously. I can't take my eyes off you and we're going to wreck."

"Okay." I turned in my seat facing the right way and re-buckled my seatbelt. I didn't pull my pants back up, though.

His sigh made it all worth it.

∞ ∞ ∞

The Sportage barely even made a bump when I pulled into my driveway. I'd intended to buy another Soul, but the salesman talked me into the SUV on the sole premise that it would be better suited for winter driving. It made sense. And it was shiny and black. I even got him to knock five-grand off the sticker price for paying in cash. His face was awesome when I handed it to him.

Jimmy pulled in behind me. I got out of the car and hit the lock button, shooting him a sultry glance over my shoulder as I practically ran to the front door.

Please don't be home. Please don't be home, I chanted in my head about Josie, as I unlocked the door and opened it.

"Josie, you home?"

Silence was the only beautiful sound in the house.

Jimmy slipped in the door behind me. He pulled off his jacket and let it fall to the floor, guiding me into the living room and pushing me down on the couch. I landed with my ass half hanging off. He knelt between my legs and leaned over me, kissing my neck with his eager lips. I could feel the hardness of him in his jeans, grinding against my sensitive flesh. I lay back and let him have a little fun first.

He lifted the front of my heavy sweater and the T-shirt beneath. I didn't wear a bra, the two heavy layers providing enough cover. He palmed both of my breasts and kissed my chest between them, planting kisses all the way down over my stomach and to the top of my pants.

He let go to pull them down. He did leave the panties on, to my surprise. I was almost glad he did. I was practically dripping. He leaned in and kissed me, right on the tiny lace bow on the front of them. And then he moved a little lower. His lips nuzzled me through the material and I became even wetter as I ground myself against his mouth.

"Oh fuck, that feels good," I said breathlessly.

"It tastes even better."

"Do I? Taste good?"

166

"Honestly, yes. I know it sounds kind of corny, but you taste like honey and strawberries." He moved his lips down to the moist center of my panties and kissed and licked. My breath came in ragged gasps.

Then my eyes narrowed as he moved back up, aiming to kiss me. I didn't know what to do, so I closed my eyes. His lips brushed against mine and I could feel the wetness coating them. My scent reached my nose and, I hate to admit it, I liked it.

"Lick your lips."

I really didn't want to, but I did. While it wasn't something that would turn me on, I didn't mind my taste. I shrugged. "I wouldn't go so far as honey and strawberries, but not bad."

"Oh, I quite enjoy it," he said and slipped his finger inside my panties, sliding inside me with complete ease. I cried out as my hips bucked against his hand.

"Jimmy!"

"Yes, Dot?"

The doorbell rang.

"Fuck."

"Want me to ignore it or see who it is?"

"See who it is, please."

"Okay, but you might want to pull your pants up."

"I'll be in the bathroom. Crying."

He kissed me on the lips, "Don't worry. We have all the time in the world," he said as he ran his fingers over the front of my panties one more time. I shuddered as he stood up.

I pulled my pants on and ran for the guest bath. It was closer, and I could hear who was at the door. Standing in front of the mirror, I heard it open and a gun fire twice. For a brief moment, I thought it was some sort of sick fucking prank until I heard Jimmy hit the floor. My scream tore open my recently healed throat.

JACQUELYN FAYE

Chapter 18

I cast a quick stone shield and ran out the bathroom door. The front door was still open, and Jimmie lay on the floor just inside. I ran for the front door, but no one was there. I dropped to the ground beside him. Two wet, red spots dotted his shirt and were spreading fast. The floor beneath him started pooling blood.

"Jimmy? Jimmy!"

He blinked and coughed blood, wheezing. The one in his upper chest must have hit a lung. The other was lower, down by his stomach. Luckily, whoever shot him hadn't gotten him in the heart or head. He wasn't dead.

"Dot," he croaked out, not quite being able to say my name.

"Shush. Don't talk."

I pulled my cell out of my sweater and dialed 911. I shouted at the operator to get me an ambulance, my friend had been shot. I spouted out my address and set the phone down. My healing skills sucked, but they were better than nothing.

I put my hands over his wounds to stop the bleeding and cast my spell. My first aid skills were abysmal. I knew with a lung wound I was supposed to do something with plastic bags and tape, but I had no clue what. I concentrated on my power and sent it into my hands. "*Tarraing an miotail as an fhoirceannadh,*" I canted as I sent tendrils of it down into his wounds. I could feel the flesh heating up as I poured the power in. Then I felt them. My power wrapped around the tiny bits of metal embedded in his flesh and pulled. I felt like a magnet.

Jimmy writhed in pain as the bullets made their way back through their respective entry points. An eternity later, I felt them touch my palms. I slowly pulled my hands away, pulling them free. He gasped, as much as he could, in relief. I tossed the bits of metal to the floor and concentrated on healing him from the inside out.

"*Leigheas an comhlacht, é a dhéanamh go hiomlán.*" I poured every bit of power I had into him to heal his wounds. I knew it wouldn't be enough, but it would buy him the precious time he needed. He would survive even if it killed me.

Jimmy, you shit, don't you fucking die on me.

I felt consciousness slip away from me and I blacked out, falling forward onto Jimmy.

A siren brought me back. I blinked, my face pressed wetly against Jimmy's shirt. I sat up and looked at him.

His face was a healthier color and he was breathing normally, if a bit raggedly. The gasping wheeze was gone. I sighed in relief and lifted his shirt. I expected two gaping wounds, but they were closed, new pink flesh was the only indication he had been wounded at all. I blinked in surprise. Healing never worked that well before for me in the past. Then again, I'd never been that desperate to save someone's life before.

Chief came in through the open door with his weapon drawn. "Where?"

"Gone. I was in the bathroom and Jimmy opened the door. I heard two gunshots and found him on the ground."

"EMTs are on their way."

"They can transport him to the hospital. I managed to get the bullets out and get him moderately healed. I don't know how well I did on the inside, though."

He holstered his weapon and knelt down, checking out the wounds. "That's going to be a little difficult to explain to the paramedics..."

"Better than a dead friend."

"Very true. Well hopefully he comes to quickly and we can find out who shot him. His pulse seems good." He let go of Jimmy's wrist. I hadn't realized he'd been checking.

"And the wheezing stopped. I freaked out when I saw it was a lung wound."

"You did a pretty amazing job healing him."

"I just don't know why they were targeting him or how they knew he'd be here."

"Either they recognized his truck in the yard, or the bullets were meant for you."

"At least they didn't blow up my new car."

"I'll check it for spells. And collect the bullets. Congrats, your house is now a crime scene."

"Joy. Don't get dust everywhere."

The sirens and screeching tires on the street out front announced the arrival of the paramedics. Chief walked over to the doorway and motioned for them to come in.

"Is that how they know there isn't a crazy gunman in here?"

"Yeah. But, there's no signal for crazy witch."

"We need to figure this out quickly. I don't want to lose anybody else."

"Me neither. I'm glad you were here to save him."

"It was my fault he was here to begin with. Chief, it's got to be somebody in our coven. They're targeting me now."

"It could be somebody targeting witches in general."

"But they're using spells."

"Well, we need to continue with the interviews. Maybe we'll get somewhere. We should call a coven meeting."

"Do it."

"Yes, Lady."

The paramedics wheeled the stretcher in the house, basically pushing us out of the way. I watched them check his vitals and the wounds and then focus their questioning stares at Chief. He pointed at me. "She used to be a nurse."

They focused their stares at me. I just shrugged. Their imaginations could fill in the gaps better than I ever could. I waited patiently as they loaded my still unconscious lover on the stretcher.

"Follow him to the hospital," Chief said behind me. "I'll get your official statement later."

"Thanks, Chief."

"You want me to call Jason?"

I thought about it for a moment. Jimmy, if he even regained consciousness, would be in the hospital for a few days at least. I could check on him before and possibly after my date. "No. But do call Dennis. Let him know what happened and to meet me at the hospital. Tell Jason to be here at seven."

"Yes, Lady." His formality was really starting to creep me out. I didn't know what was behind it and I didn't like it. Subservient men weren't my thing.

"You okay, Chief?"

"No. But we'll discuss it later when your friend hasn't been shot. Just don't like feeling helpless."

"I feel you. No more calling me Lady, though."

He shrugged. "You know, that works both ways, right?"

I sighed. He had me there. "Thank you, *Bill.*"

He nodded and I followed the EMTs out the door, following them all the way to the hospital and trying very *hard* not to cry.

∞ ∞ ∞

"What happened?"

I found myself getting tired of the question. A little normalcy would be nice. Or at least not having to explain

172

who died, who blew up, or who got shot. It was getting tedious.

Dennis had skidded to a stop in front of Jimmy's bed in the emergency room. I was sitting next to the bed, just holding his hand. He hadn't woken up yet.

"He was at my house and answered my door. Somebody shot him twice before taking off."

He stepped in the cordoned off area and leaned a little closer to me. "So, they gave up on the spells and went straight to guns?"

"Yes."

"What happened to your face?"

"They spelled my car to explode."

"That was you?"

I nodded. Apparently, if you wanted to avoid the town gossip, one only had to pull a few shifts at the firehouse.

"Jesus, Dot. I'm glad you're okay. How's Jimmy?"

"I got the bullets out and healed him as much as I could before the medics showed up. Doc said, and I quote, it's almost as if he hadn't been shot at all."

"Then why is he not awake?"

"I have a theory, but I'm not really certain."

"What?"

"Shock and energy. He went into shock from the amount of damage he took. He went into shock from having the damage repaired in a few minutes. And while I poured all of my power into him, he still had to use all of his own to actually heal. It was a team effort. I normally suck at healing."

"If the doc says he couldn't even tell he was shot, I would say you need to rethink your opinion on your skills."

"I couldn't do it again. I've never dumped so much power into anything. I just *really* didn't want him to die." And just like that all the raw emotion I'd been pushing away to keep myself together flooded through me. My chest tightened as the tears fell.

He smiled. "You fell for him, didn't you?"

"Maybe. A little. He has a certain charm."

Dennis chuckled and pulled the other chair a little closer to me before sitting down. I leaned against him with a weary sigh. He pulled me close and just comforted me.

It was when the tears hit my leggings that I realized how much I already cared about Jimmy. He'd become an integral part of my life, a life I couldn't imagine without him in. I may have already fallen in love with the bastard.

"Shh. He's going to be okay."

"I know."

"Then why are you crying?"

"Because I almost lost him."

"Luckily, whoever shot him had terrible aim."

"Or they were surprised it wasn't me."

"I'm starting to think they're just trying to take out the whole coven."

I sat up straighter. "Why?"

"Who knows. Maybe it's a witch hunter or something."

"Who uses magic?"

"Hmm. Maybe not."

"Dennis, it *has* to be somebody in the coven. Can you think of anything that Richie, Dane, and Chief's wife have in common?"

"Other than being in the coven? No."

Something wasn't sitting right. There had to be a connection. My mother's words floated back to me. Ask people *outside* the coven. One place to start popped into my head. "Tell-a-Marge."

"What?"

"Nothing. You gonna be here a while?"

"Yeah. I'm off duty now."

"Sweet. When he wakes up, call me. Please?"

"Sure thing. Where you heading?"

"A date and some investigative work."

"A date?"

"Yeah. Jason."

"Huh. I wouldn't have been shocked if you'd said the chief…"

"We have a date on Friday." I chuckled at the absurdity of it all.

"Who?"

"Chief and I."

He cocked an eyebrow.

"Don't look at me like that. They all know."

"I didn't say anything," he said with a mischievous grin.

"No, but I don't like the tone of your thoughts." I winked and patted him on the shoulder. "Seriously, call me when he wakes up."

"Will do. Have fun with…Jason."

"He's not that bad."

"No. Just angry at the world."

"I know. It's why I asked him out."

Chapter 19

"You sure you want to do this tonight?"

I nodded, starting the car and putting my seatbelt on. "Jimmy's going to be fine. I already postponed on you once and felt horrible."

"Um, getting blown up is a perfectly acceptable excuse."

"I know. But I was really looking forward to our date."

"Why?" He cocked and eyebrow, and with his angular face it made him look more Vulcan than human. He just needed some pointed ears.

I put the car in reverse but didn't take my foot off the brake. I didn't know why I'd been looking forward to our date. I really didn't. I shrugged. "I don't know. Don't get me wrong, you're a gorgeous guy, but it was something else."

"Well, I think we can rule out my charming personality."

"Honestly, I think that was it."

"Huh?"

"Once I sat down to *really* talk to you, you were someone else. Someone hurt, someone shy, but actually quite alluring. Don't sell yourself short, Jason. You might have been angry at the world, but once you drop all that, I don't know. I'm rambling. Feel free to stop me."

"No." He chuckled.

"Okay. Well let's hear about you. Tell me what there is to know about the alluring Jason." I backed out of the driveway and pointed us toward the diner.

"Not much to tell. I was always Rebecca's little brother. We had the same mother, but different fathers. We couldn't be more different if we hadn't been siblings."

"Were your parents all witches?"

"No. Becca's father was. Mine was human."

"Is your mom still around?"

"Alive, yes. In town, no. Once I turned eighteen, she moved to New England."

"How long ago was that?"

"Twenty years or so."

"How old was your sister when she died?"

"Fifty-something."

"Everybody in this coven is so *young*. I guess that's a hazard of the humans around you not knowing what you are." I felt a little out of place.

"Not Dwight. He's over three-hundred."

"He's young compared to my mother."

"Wow. Really?"

"Yeah. Mother moved to this country in the early 1800s. Ireland for more than a few centuries before that. She's seen some shit."

"How old are you?"

"I'll be a hundred next year."

"Wow."

"You're not earning any points."

He chuckled. "You're way older than Bill but act so young. Most of the time," he added thoughtfully.

"Yeah, yeah. I don't wanna grow up." I found a parking space right in front of the Diner.

"Huh. Haven't been here in ages."

"They have really good food."

"I remember."

"You don't eat out much?"

"I don't go out much. Work and home."

"You should consider burning that place. Buy a house in town while the market sucks."

"I was planning on it. Once I saved enough."

"Thinking ahead. I like that."

I opened my door and we headed inside. The place was busier than usual. "Dot!"

Margie practically ran across the floor of the diner as fast as her older frame could carry her. It looked more like a shuffle than a run. She threw her arms around me. The patrons of the diner glanced up in confusion. "Heard about the shooting. Is Jimmy okay?"

I was a little surprised she knew him, but then again, I doubted there was a soul living in Cedar Falls that she *didn't* know. "He's going to be fine."

"If it weren't for bad luck, girl, you wouldn't have *any* at all."

"There's more truth to that than you know. Thanks, Marge."

"Sit. Coke?"

"Yes, please."

"And for you? Jason? Is that you?"

He nodded shyly.

"You haven't aged a–" She stopped saying what she was going to say. "What would you like to drink, kiddo?"

Jason chuckled. "I'll have a Coke, too, please."

She shuffled off and since my usual booth was taken, we sat down at one of the tables. Jason took the seat closest to me instead of on the other side.

"She knows," Jason chuckled softly.

"Yeah. Her husband is the coroner. I'm sure he's seen all sorts of weird shit."

"Especially since you came to town. Things have gotten interesting."

"Wonder why that is?"

"You did bring the coven back together. We'd hardly seen each other in two years?"

"Huh. I hadn't thought of that. But why kill me?"

"Because you're too beautiful? Maybe it's a jealous woman."

"Uh huh. Sure."

"Ask any one. You are probably one of the most gorgeous women I've ever seen." He said it while perusing the menu. Almost as an afterthought.

It didn't stop me from blushing.

We ordered and ate. Talked and laughed. By the time we were done, we were some of the last people in the dinner. Marge finally brought our check. I grabbed it before Jason could. "You're saving for a house," I said, leaving little room for argument. "Besides, I asked you out."

"Fine. Pushy *and* beautiful."

"You have no idea."

Marge came to pick up the check. "Hey, Marge, got a minute?"

"Sure, sweetie. What's up?"

"Sit."

She pulled out one of the chairs and parked herself. "Whatcha need?"

"Just a question or two. Did you know Richie? The fireman who died in the truck last week?"

"Yeah. Sad. He was good friends with the fellow who got shot, right?"

I nodded. "Did you know Dane, the policeman who was murdered?"

"Yes. He came in here for Chief all the time. Picking up food. He ate here quite often, too."

"What about Jason's sister?"

"Her and Chief ate here more than you."

"Can you think of *anything* the three of them had in common?"

She leaned forward across the table. "Other than being like you two?"

I nodded, stifling a giggle.

"No. Not a thing. The two boys I saw with the same woman, but Rebecca was always with the chief."

"Which woman?"

"Don't know her name, but she was always dressed to the nines and real pretty."

"If you remember her name, let me know?"

"Sure thing. This about the murders?"

"Just trying to figure out why someone is doing these horrible things."

"Sad. You all might be a little different, and Herb always warned me not to pry, but good people are good people."

I was a little surprised. Marge had a gossip problem. How she wasn't blabbing about us to the entire town would remain a mystery. I'm surprised there weren't headlines in the paper. "Thanks, Marge."

She nodded and took the check up to the register.

"Well, that wasn't exactly helpful. Nothing in common with the three of them. Or you."

"Well. I might just be an added target, since I did bring the coven back. Maybe they liked things the way they were."

"Why not just leave the coven?"

"Who knows. I'd believe anything at this point. *You*, just make sure you stay safe. Okay?"

"Yes, Ma'am."

I let the ma'am part go. "Come on. Let's get out of here. I want to go check on Jimmy before the night is over."

He slid his chair back and offered me a hand. I let him help me up. It had been a long couple of days. "Is it bad that I like it that you're worried about me?" He gave me a small smile.

"Nope."

"This was… This was more fun than I've had in years. Would you mind doing this with me again sometime? But you have to let me buy next time."

"I'd love to."

He took my hand in his and brought it to his lips, giving me a gentle kiss on the back of the hand. I squeezed his. He was really a nice kid. I was glad he had given up his anger toward me.

We drove back to my house in relative silence. I shut off the engine and got out. "I'm going to head home," he said softly.

"Okay. I'm going to see if Josie is home and then head to the hospital before visiting hours are over." I looked at his rusted car. "Call me…if you break down."

"Bessie is a beast. She wouldn't do that to me."

"Uh huh. Good night, Jason," I said sweetly and walked over to him, giving him a soft kiss on his cheek.

"Night, Dot. Thanks again."

He headed to his car and I headed toward my door. A bad feeling washed over me as I spun, just as he started it. The engine rumbled to life and he put it in gear, pulling away quite loudly. I let go of the breath I'd been holding, keeping my eyes on him until he made it around the corner. I needed to start playing it safer. Especially with my people.

I sent a tendril of power at my front door and found nothing out of the ordinary. Hopefully the murderer hadn't given up on magic and invested in some claymore mines. I wasn't quite sure I could detect those. I went to unlock the door and it opened, a horrified Josie standing there.

"What the fuck, Dot?"

"What, what the fuck?"

"I came home to a crime scene."

"Gotcha beat. I was in the crime scene."

She threw her arms around me and hugged me like she hadn't seen me in a decade or two. I patted her on the back, wanting nothing more than to continue, but I needed to hurry to get to the hospital. "I gotta run. Visiting hours at the hospital end at nine. I want to check on Jimmy."

"Okay, but I'm going with you. Consider me your sidekick until this is all over. I'm not leaving you alone at all. Not even to pee."

"Okay, but I draw the line at number two."

"Deal."

"Holy shit, is that a new car?"

"Technically, it's a SUV, but yes. That's what started this whole mess."

"Chief filled me in. I'm sorry."

"I'm okay. Jimmy, not so much. Two to the chest."

"I know. Chief said you healed him?"

"Almost completely. I have no idea how. I've always sucked at it."

"You just wanna take my job." I keyed open the car and we slipped inside. She glanced around appreciatively and whistled. "Nice."

"Thanks."

"I really need to get a car."

"You should." We pulled out of the driveway and I turned on the radio, resting my head in my hand against the driver door. "So, no Candace tonight?"

"She works at night. That's why I only get to see her during the day. She's off on the weekends, though."

"Why don't you invite her for dinner?"

"I will. Which one of your guys are you going to invite?"

"Har har har. I only have the one."

"So, where did you go tonight?"

"Dinner."

"With?"

"Jason…"

"What you up to tomorrow?"

"Dinner."

"With?"

"Shut your face, Josie."

She cackled all the way to the hospital.

Chapter 20

"How you feeling?"

Jimmy rolled his eyes.

"Sure. Go ahead. Roll your eyes at me. I'm just glad you can." I was sitting in the chair next to his bed, leaning forward on my arms. Jimmy needed a shower, but I didn't care.

"Doc says they might release him tomorrow," Dennis chimed in from the seat next to Josie.

"You shush. You're still in trouble. You were supposed to let me know when he woke up."

"Don't look at me. He was the one who stopped me."

I shot Jimmy a dirty look. He shrugged. "Sorry."

"I'll forgive you if you got a good look at the bastard that did this to you."

"No. He was wearing a mask. I didn't even get a good look at that. I opened the door and he pulled the trigger."

"But it was a guy?"

"Yeah."

That narrowed our list of suspects to half the town and half the coven. I sighed in aggravation. I was hoping he had seen more. I was hoping he could have put a stop to this hellish nightmare.

"Sorry, Dot."

I patted his hand. "Not your fault. I don't even think it was your fault you got shot. I think those bullets were meant for me."

"Then I'm glad it happened."

If he wasn't lying in a hospital bed and in massive amounts of pain, I would have hit him. Or kissed him. I wasn't quite sure how I felt about it. Instead I narrowed my eyes at him.

"Boop," he said and poked my nose.

Reaching over to touch his hip, I whispered, "*Pléisiúr.*"

His eyes widened as he spasmed a little. I'd sent a jolt of pure pleasure into him. It was a handy little trick and fun at parties. I noticed the blanket covering his lower half twitch a little.

"That was mean."

"You booped my nose."

"I'm gonna boop your ass when I get out of here."

"Promise?"

The look on his face was worth the blush on my cheeks. Especially when Dennis gasped.

Josie simply said, "Rawr."

The same doctor that had treated me for third degree explosions walked into the room studying something intently. He didn't even notice the crowd in the room.

"I just don't understand this. Other than some serious scarring marking the passage of the bullet, you're completely fine. It might take you some time to work the stiffness out of your chest muscles, but… Yeah. I've got nothing." He looked up from what he'd been reading and saw me sitting next to his patient.

"I think I just found the cause of your extraordinary luck, Mr. Duncan."

"Hi, Doc."

"Good evening, Miss Blackwell."

"Dot, please."

He opened his mouth to say something but stopped. "Miss Dot, could you… Would you mind coming with me for a moment?"

I sighed. This wasn't going to end well. A lot of people accepted weird things as just that. Then there was the other half of the population that absolutely *hated* inexplicable things. They needed to debunk myths and blame everything on photoshop. It helped them sleep better at night.

"Sure, Doc." I stood up, giving Jimmy a quick kiss on his forehead.

"Want me to come with you?"

I shook my head at Josie. I kind of had a feeling this was going to happen sooner or later. Hell, I'd expected it to happen with the paramedics, but they did their job and rolled their eyes.

As soon as we were in the hall, the doc pulled the door shut and stared at me. "I'm sure you must be aware of what is going through my head right now."

"That there were two miracles in two days?"

"Sort of. But you see, Dot, the one commonality between those two miracles just happens to be…you."

"You think I'm some sort of miracle worker?"

"No. I'm *hoping* you are."

"Pardon?" I blinked in surprise. That hadn't been the answer I'd been expecting.

"I have another gunshot victim down in the ER…"

I saw where he was going with this. I held up my hand. "Doc. You're misunderstanding something. While I admit that it would *seem* like I *might* have had something to do with this, I can assure you I *didn't*."

Back in Ashville, most of the townspeople knew that witches lived among them. We even had a huge population of witches. My former coven had over seventy members. Witches from far and wide migrated there as a sort of sanctuary. It became almost a symbiotic relationship, and the head of that organism was my *very* charismatic mother. When she wasn't hexing assholes onto people's foreheads. Halloween in Ashville had become a major holiday, rivaling Christmas in scope.

This was Cedar Falls. Witch population had dwindled down to a mere eleven and threatened to get smaller every day. There was *no way* in the seven hells I was going to out myself to a perfect stranger. I felt bad for the person in the ER with the bullet wound but...

"It's a six-year-old girl. Her brother was playing with the gun he found in daddy's closet. The bullet pierced the back of her skull. It's was a relatively small round, or she would have had two holes in her skull. We can't go in and get it because if we do, her brain will swell to twice the size. If we don't remove it, she's going to die anyway."

"Shit."

"So, you can see why I'm looking for that miracle right now. If I was wrong, I apologize."

"You are...n't."

I almost waited for him to shout, "Ha!"

He didn't. He closed his eyes and whispered, "Oh, thank God."

"Doc. This goes to your grave, okay. Maybe one day you'll know all about it, but I will help you this once. *If* I can. I'm not making any promises, though."

"Dot, the girl was dead or brain-dead either way. I won't even say anything to anyone to get their hopes up. Fuck, I'll even dress you up like a nurse to get you into that room."

"Is her brain going to swell after I pull the bullet out?"

"There is a high probability. Why?"

"I saw an episode of a show where they pulled a pencil out of a kid's brain through his eye and he died from it."

"Medical dramas are highly intensified with scenarios. I usually laugh when I see them, but I'm not going to lie. It can happen."

"What if I told you I wasn't the only one who could do this. Let's say I pulled the bullet out slowly and another person healed the brain as it came out... Would that be better?"

"You can't do both at the same time?"

"No."

"Then, yes. It would be."

"Get two sets of scrubs. Same size. Meet me back here in a couple of minutes."

He didn't question, he didn't break down and thank me, he took off running.

I sighed and hoped I'd made the right decision. I'd practically handed my and Josie's ass to the doctor on a platter. If it weren't a little kid going to die, I probably wouldn't have. But Josie and I could always run. The rest of the witches in town...not so much.

I went back into Jimmy's room and all three were staring at me. "Paging, Nurse Josie. Nurse Josie to the ER, please."

"What?"

I gave them a brief rundown of what had transpired in the hallway. Josie looked worried, Dennis looked shocked, and Jimmy looked proud. He rubbed my back as I sat back down next to him while we waited for the doctor.

He slipped into the room and handed me two sets of scrubs. "I'll be out in the hall. Come out after you've changed and make sure you wear the masks. All the nurses at the hospital *know* each other. You two will stick out like sore thumbs. Walk behind me, I'll cover any questions."

"Okay, Doc. You realize how much we are putting on the line right now, right?"

"I do. Trust me. This stays between us. I could lose my license if this goes bad, but I'm at the point where I don't care. That little girl didn't ask for this."

I nodded, feeling the same way.

I stood up and stripped, pulling the scrubs on. Jimmy didn't hide his stares. Dennis was polite and turned around. He'd seen both of us naked before, so I shrugged. Dennis was a gentleman.

"Perv," I whispered to Jimmy.

He wiggled his eyebrows.

"We'll be back," I said and headed out of the room, Josie right behind me.

"Coven healer, huh?"

"Yep. I'll get you a nametag."

"With sparkles, please. Maybe a unicorn."

The doctor didn't say anything to us, just led us to the elevator. He held up a keycard and hit the button for the first floor after the sensor *beeped.*

"I'll handle the bullet, *slowly.* You dump as much healing into her little head as she and you can handle. Good plan?"

"Good plan."

"What kind of healing? What kind of power?" The doctor seemed genuinely interested. "Better question is what are you?"

"Witches and magic, Doc. Real honest to goodness, turn you into a toad, stir big cauldron witches. You wanted to know, now you do. We're real. And we're not new age witches, either. My mother is six-hundred-years-old. I'm nearly a hundred. Josie is the same age as me. Now you know why we like to keep a low profile..."

He looked skeptical but nodded his head.

"So, are you going to dance and chant?"

"You'll be in the room with us in case it doesn't go as planned. It's easier to show than tell."

The door *dinged,* and he headed straight to the ICU ward of the ER. He donned a mask from his pocket and walked us straight into her room, closing the door behind us.

"This is Makayla."

The little girl was lying on her stomach on the bed, her head tilted to the side with an oxygen mask strapped to her face. The wound on the back of her head had been shaved and slathered in a yellow liquid, I tried not to look inside the wound. I could feel dinner threatening to rear its ugly head.

"Lady bless."

"Pray to whomever will help," he said somberly.

"I'm going to have to touch the wound directly. With my skin. Is that okay?"

"Dot, an infection is the *least* of this girl's worries right now. Wash your hands in the sink over there first, but I'm not too worried about it. Mr. Duncan didn't get an infection."

I nodded. Josie and I both scrubbed our hands anyway.

"I'll go first and touch the wound. You put your hands on her head and heal like a level seventy cleric. Got it?"

"Yes, Lady."

Josie had gone into serious mode. The severity of what we were about to do *really* sank in. "Lady guide us," I whispered.

I put my fingers over the hole, gently.

"*Tarraing an miotail as an fhoirceannadh,*" I said and let a tendril of my power enter the wound. After more than a few moments, I could feel it. It had entered the back of her head and angled up, emerging on the top of her brain, wedged against the inside of her skull. I could feel her in there, too. There was some damage, but I could still feel that light that was *her.* She was curious as to what I was doing, and I sent her a mental wink. I could hear her laughter all around me.

"Sweet, sweet girl," I said aloud in the room.

I wrapped my power around the tiny piece of metal and pulled. It took a moment before it started moving slowly, back the way it had gone in. "I've got it, Josie. It's moving. Start."

It started as a soft glow around me. I wasn't the bullet, but I was the power wrapped around it. Everything around me filled my senses and Josie's power wrapped us in warmth. I could feel it tickling Makayla. I'm sure I was smiling back in the little room.

Slowly, I pulled, giving Josie plenty of time to close the channel as we passed through it, almost like a zipper. *Finally*, I felt metal with my fingers. I opened my eyes and saw the glint of it under the lamp above us. I didn't stop, drawing it through the hole in her skull until the tip slipped free. I dropped it on the bed next to her and let Josie work her magic.

"That was the most incredible thing I've ever seen."

I wanted to say, "Thank you," but just like before, I passed out.

Chapter 21

I came to in a private room, Josie in the bed next to me. I groaned in exhaustion. I hadn't thought about the chance of me passing out after expending all that power. I hope I didn't land on Makayla.

I sat up and shook Josie. "Wake up."

"Did you get the license plate?"

"Of what?"

"That fucking semi."

I laughed. If she was okay to crack jokes, she was fine.

"Good work, " I told her and patted her leg.

"You owe me food. Lots of food. And ice-cream."

"You're cheap."

"You know it."

The door opened. I jumped in surprise, but it was just the doctor. "Congratulations, Makayla woke up before you two."

"She okay?"

His nod and his smile were music to my eyeballs. "You guys want jobs? I *seriously* wouldn't mind you putting me out of business."

"If you could feel how we feel right now, you wouldn't be asking. It's like a hangover. From schnapps."

"That bad?"

"Yeah. And it feels like a dehydrated grizzly shit in my mouth. Got any water?"

"I can do better. Maybe some electrolytes will help."

He slipped out of the room and came back with a clear plastic jug and two cups. He splashed some in each one and handed them to us. I downed mine and held it out for more. It wasn't bad. "What is that?"

"Pedialyte. It's like Gatorade without the coloring and corn syrup."

Almost immediately I felt a little better. I downed the second cup and had risen to sub-human. "That's pretty cool. I might have to stock up on that."

"Science meets magic. Whoda thunkit."

"How did we get here?"

"Your nice fireman friend and a blonde nurse who seemed to know you."

"Blonde nurse?"

"Candace," Josie said. "She works here."

"She's a nurse?"

"Yeah."

"Why didn't you say something?"

"Hey, Dot. My future girlfriend is a nurse. There."

"Girlfriend?" The doctor seemed intrigued.

"Long story."

"Well, she went and got your fireman friend. And we brought you here. Don't worry, nurses sometimes pass out. Nobody thought anything of it."

I nodded and shrugged, too tired to care anymore. I lay back on the bed and closed my eyes.

I heard voices around me but didn't pay attention, drifting in and out. I don't think I'd ever been that tired in my life. When lips pressed against mine... That woke me up. I didn't open my eyes though. I just melted into the kiss.

Then I realized it wasn't Jimmy.

I pushed him away slowly until his face came into focus. Chief was hovering over me and gave me a soft smile. "What are you doing?"

"Well, isn't it customary to wake a sleeping princess with a kiss?"

"Pretty sure that's illegal in forty-nine states..."

He had the sense to look embarrassed. "Dot. I'm sorry. I didn't think you would mind."

"I didn't. I'm just glad it was you."

"Are you?"

I thought about it before nodding. "Yeah. Trust me, I enjoyed it."

"Thank the Lady. Now I don't have to arrest myself."

"Hmm. Maybe you should. I wouldn't mind having you in handcuffs for a little while…"

I made *him* blush. "I heard about your new side job." I opened my mouth to defend myself. "Don't. I'm glad you did it. Not only did you save the little girl, you saved the family. If she'd died… I don't even want to think how that would go. The father even turned in his handgun to be destroyed."

"Really?"

"Yeah. He was a pretty avid gun nut, too. You should see the stickers on his truck. I'd imagine they'll be the next to go."

"So how did the doctor explain her recovery?"

Chief sat down next to the bed. "Said he walked into the room and an angel was standing over their daughter. She reached right in and pulled the bullet out."

"No, he didn't."

"Yes, he did. See, that's the thing with magic and miracles. You have to preach to the crowd. He knew what would sell and what wouldn't. Mr. Akin and his family were far more likely to believe in the power of angels than the sexy witch in room 118."

I blushed. "I can see that. Damn angels, taking all my credit."

"Credit you never wanted…"

"Nope. Let the angels keep it."

"What really sold them is the little girl remembering the sweet angel in her head. She said the angel tickled her and kept her warm."

I blushed again. Right before I started crying. At least they were happy tears. That was a nice change.

"Where'd everybody go?"

"Josie went off with Candace. The doctor gave her the rest of the night off to see Josie home safely. I think he might have been playing matchmaker there. You made a new friend. Doc Shapiro is a good one to have."

"My third human friend in town."

"You should make more. Lot of good people in this town."

"I noticed that. I'll try."

He nodded. "You need a ride?"

"I don't think so. I'm good now that I had some electrolytes and a nap."

"Okay. I'll let Jimmy know you're heading home. Visiting hours are over."

"Where's Dennis?"

"With Jimmy. He's going to keep an eye on him tonight. I told Candace to stay with Josie until you got home. You might want to keep her there tonight though, and not for nefarious reasons. I don't think any of us should be alone. I even dragged Dwight out of the woods to stay at Jason's."

"That's pretty smart."

"Thanks. I have my moments."

"Unless one of them is the killer."

"But then we'll *know*."

"That's pretty fucking morbid, Chief."

"Thanks. I have my moments. Come on. I'll walk you to your car and test it for incendiary spells."

"Thanks. I don't think I could magic open a door lock right now."

He stood up and scooped me up off the bed. I squeaked and threw my arms around his neck. "I can walk you know."

"I know. But this is much more fun."

"I'm *heavy*."

"Yeah, you are. You need to quit eating at the diner…"

"Chief Dick, if you think—"

He silenced me with another kiss.

∞ ∞ ∞

I unlocked my front door without checking for magic. Josie and Candace would have done it already. Walking into my living room, two heads popped up over the back of the couch. They were lying next to each other, watching a Christmas movie.

"Just me," I called out.

"Welcome home."

"Welcome back, Lady."

I walked over and plopped my ass down in the love seat. "It's Dot, Candace."

They were lying under a blanket. Candace was in front of Josie, being the little spoon. Not that she had much choice. The girl couldn't big spoon a teaspoon. I briefly wondered how she treated patients at the hospital. Unless she stashed a step stool in every room.

She ran to the kitchen and returned with a glass of white wine. I got a little shock when she handed it to me. "Uh, thanks."

She smiled and nodded, crawling back under the blanket.

"How you feeling?" Josie looked at me over the arm of the sofa.

"Better after the cat nap. Chief told me he's pairing everybody up until the killings are over. Glad you two made it safe."

"Yeah. The doc was nice enough to give Candace the rest of the night off."

I could hear Josie *pretending* to be shocked. I chuckled a little into my wine.

"Do you live alone, Candace?"

She tore her eyes from the movie and looked up at me. The girl's eyes were too large for her face. She almost looked like an anime character. "Yes."

"Stay here tonight, if you don't mind. I agree with Chief. Nobody stays alone."

"Thank you."

"You're not the killer, are you?" I said half-jokingly.

"No, Lady."

Well that makes me feel a lot safer.

Josie shot me an angry look.

"I was kidding!"

Candace poked Josie in the ribs. "She is wise to ask. She does not know me."

"I was giving her a look for the stupidity of the question. Like a killer is going to admit to being a killer. Let's just hold a coven meeting and ask everybody."

"That might not be a bad idea. The Chief is planning on interviewing everybody anyway," Candace answered deadpan.

I shrugged. "At least we would get it out of the way. I'm tired of getting blown up, shot at, and if I lose another witch, I'm going to torch the whole damn town."

Candace looked over at me a little fearful. "You feel that strongly about us?"

I gulped but nodded. "Yes. You're my damn coven. I'm supposed to protect you. Instead my boyfriend got shot protecting me. If I find out who is responsible for all of this... The Lady as my witness, I will rain hellfire down upon them and scorch them from this earth."

Candace didn't look afraid. She looked happy.

"What?" I asked her.

"Just happy. The last high priestess was very nice, but she didn't feel like you do. She was too enamored with her husband. We were a broken coven long before her murder."

"That's just sad. Love is supposed to make you better, not consume you."

"That's very wise."

"I have my moments. Mostly not, but there are some." I took a sip of my wine. It wasn't overly sweet. I kind of liked it. "I'm hungry. Do we have any chips and salsa?"

"No. And nothing in this house either. I looked." Josie sounded a little grumpy.

"Guess I should replace the fridge and do some shopping, huh?"

"I'll make you a deal. You buy the fridge and I'll stock it."

"Nah. I got it. I'll order one from the Depot and have it delivered. I'll just do the whole appliance package. I meant to do it the other day, just never seem to have the time..."

"I know, sweetie. I'm grumpy because I'm hungry and nothing is open in this town this late."

"Want me to run to the gas station?"

"No. I'm tired anyway. It's way past my bedtime."

"Then I'll order appliances in the morning and take you guys to the diner for breakfast. Deal?"

"Deal," Josie answered happily.

"Lady, you do not need to buy me breakfast."

"Go to sleep, Candace. Don't argue."

"Yes, Lady."

Chapter 22

Waking up and realizing you're not alone while a murderer is on the loose was more terrifying than I would have expected...

I screamed and sat up, flipping the comforter off me, Josie *and* Candace were sound asleep on either side of me. Sometime during the night, they had crawled into bed with me and curled around me like a couple of puppies. They both screamed and looked up at me.

"What?" Josie yelled.

"Nothing. You scared me."

"The frigging heater went out. We woke you up when we came in here last night. You lifted the covers and told us to get in and shut up."

"Yeah. I don't remember that."

Candace didn't say a word, just buried her face back in my tummy and hugged my leg. I sighed and laid back down, running my fingers through her hair. She really was a puppy. I imagined her with a tail, wagging furiously.

"What's wrong with the heat?"

"I don't know. The thermostat says it's on, but it's not making the usual noise."

"I'll call a repairman. It's probably as old as the house. Why didn't you just magic your room to be warm?"

"This was more fun," Josie answered.

I laughed and ran my fingers through her hair, as well. She snuggled against me, too. "There's just one flaw in your logic."

"What?"

"I have to pee. Let me up."

"Noooo. Five more minutes."

"You're going to get wet."

"Kinky."

"Ew, Josie. That's gross."

She just chuckled and rolled over, letting me get up. Candace must have been listening, she let go of my leg and lifted her head off my stomach. That took a lot of the pressure off, but not enough. I slipped off the end of the bed and ran into my bathroom. The linoleum was freezing.

It was early, too early to call a repair company. I needed to grab some socks out of my dresser. Next time I was in town, I needed to buy some slippers.

I flushed and pulled my pajama shorts back up. Stopping to wash my hands, I noticed my face had completely healed. I breathed a sigh of relief. No more raccoon eyes.

"Anybody want a pair of socks?" I called out as I entered the bedroom.

"Wearing them."

"No thank you, Lady."

I grabbed a pair and sat on the edge of the bed, pulling them on. "Get up, lazy butts. I'm hungry."

Josie groaned, and Candace sat up, rubbing her eyes with her palms. She really was too cute. The tips of her ears poked through her hair. "Any faerie blood in your family, Candace?"

She nodded but didn't elaborate.

"Really?" Josie asked her.

"Yes." She stopped rubbing her eyes and looked up at her, shyly.

"Don't look at me like that. That's awesome. And *really* rare. I've seen true elves before, they visited the coven back home. I've never met a witch with faerie blood though."

"You don't hate it?"

"Hell no. That's friggin' cool."

I couldn't even begin to describe the look of relief on her face. She looked like she was about to cry. My gut told me Candace had a much harder life than we could imagine. I made a mental note to ask her about it sometime. She looked over and shot me a questioning look.

Instead of telling her it didn't bother me, I scooted closer to her and gave her a hug. This time she did cry a little. "You are *always* welcome in our home. Got it?"

She nodded against me.

I let her go and headed into the kitchen to order appliances. Grabbing my phone from where I'd left it plugged in to charge next to my laptop, I glanced at the screen. I'd missed a bunch of calls from Freddy Johnson over the past two days. He even called again that morning. Instead of listening to the message, I dialed him back.

He picked up on the first ring. "Johnson Brothers."

"Morning, Freddy. Sorry I missed your calls."

He chuckled. "That's okay, Miss Blackwell. Heard you had some *difficulties.*"

"Yeah. You could say that. So, what's the bad news?"

"Well, I've got your estimate."

"Lemme hear it."

He told me. I whistled. It was almost double than what I'd been expecting.

"Yeah. The scope of work is quite large. I can cut back on the quality of some of the materials and requote you."

I thought about it.

In for a penny, in for a pound.

"Will this be the bookstore I've always dreamt of?"

"Probably, and more."

"Do it. How long?"

"One week to demolish. Probably two to three months and you'll be set to open."

"Then get to work, Mr. Johnson," I added lightheartedly.

"Will do."

"Need me to drop off a check?"

"Need you to sign off on the quote first, then a deposit. Then if you want to take out a construction loan, it can be set up to pay in increments as the work is completed."

"No loan. I have funds available."

"Then a deposit check for ten percent. You can pay as we go."

"Sounds good. I'll be at the Cedar Falls Diner in about an hour, I can bring my checkbook if you'll be in the area."

"See you there."

The line clicked dead and I smiled. That was one thing I could knock off my list. I needed to find a book vendor and ten million other little things, but at least the store was finally going to be a reality.

I opened my laptop and went to the Depot's website. I quickly migrated to the appliance package section and clicked the one I liked. Black stainless-steel would look nice. I paid and set up delivery, knocking a second thing off my list. It had already been a productive morning…

∞ ∞ ∞

"I need a steak omelet and some pancakes."

Marge stared at me over her check pad. "You're not going with the usual?"

"No. My body says I need a steak omelet. Who am I to argue?"

She laughed and wrote it down. "What about you, Josie?"

"What is scrapple?"

"If you don't know, I wouldn't order it."

"Um. Okay?"

"Picture a pig's insides, ground up into a loaf, sliced, and fried."

"I'll have what Dot's having…" It was the first time I'd seen Josie turn green.

"Good choice. I told Herb not to put that shit on the menu. We have like three people a year order it. Mostly on a dare. Stinks up the whole damn diner."

"What about for you?"

Candace seemed unsure. "Fruit crepes?"

"Good choice. I'll have your food out shortly."

"Do you eat meat?" Josie asked Candace.

"I have. I don't care for it, though."

I smiled when they weren't looking. They sat next to each other on the other side of the booth. They really did make a cute couple. Candace took a sip of her tea and leaned against Josie. I wasn't sure if it was a sign of affection or if she just wanted her warmth. I don't think Josie cared, either way.

The chime over the door rang and my contractor walked in.

"Hey, Freddy."

"Morning, Miss Blackwell."

"If you don't call me Dot, I'm not signing."

He gave his deep earthy chuckle. "Morning, Dot."

"Much better. Sit. Coffee?"

"No, thank you. I really do need to run." He opened a manila folder and set it and a pen from his shirt pocket in front of me. I signed it, dated it, and handed it back to him. My checkbook-slash-wallet and phone were sitting on the table in front of me. I'd never been a fan of purses. I flipped it open and tore out the check I'd written out to him at the house. He looked at it, nodded, and slipped it in the folder with the quote. "Pleasure to do business with you, ma'am."

"Do you want the key?"

"If you have it on you."

I reached into my pocket and pulled out my ring, sliding the key off and handing it to him.

"*Now*, I'm off. The demolition crew will start tomorrow. Have a dumpster coming in."

"Have fun."

"Oh, I will. I'm looking forward to this."

"Not as much as I am."

He nodded, tipped his hat, and lumbered back out the door.

"How much did that cost you?" Josie sounded sad.

"Only ten percent down."

"Which is?"

"Still a lot."

"What are you going to name it?" Candace shyly asked.

"First Moon Books."

Their expressions told me I'd picked *exactly* the right name.

∞ ∞ ∞

"You're sure I'm not hurting you?"

"You could lay on top of me and it wouldn't hurt. You're fine, I promise."

I was nestled into Jimmy's side, lying on his bed. It felt a little strange to be in the house he shared with Dennis. I'd been so excited when I'd gotten his call, I drove right over after dropping Candace and Josie back at the house.

He had a flat screen television mounted to the wall and was watching some movie about really tall blue people on another planet. It was entertaining, but I didn't want to start watching from the middle of the movie. I was more there for snuggling. He was home. He was alive. I was very, very happy. Ecstatic even. I buried my face in his chest and closed my eyes. He even showered.

"You okay?"

I nodded without looking up. "Just glad you're home."

"You and me both. Doc kept coming into my room to ask me questions about you."

That concerned me a little. "You didn't tell him you're a witch, did you?"

"No. But I think he has his suspicions."

"Great. Do the guy a favor..."

"No. Don't worry about it. I think he's just trying to piece together everything in his head. I mean what you did... That was epic. I'm very proud of you. I think Doc Shapiro wants to start the First Church of Dot."

"That scares me even more."

"Not me. I know I'd be first in line to worship at your feet."

"You have a foot fetish?"

"Honestly, I couldn't think of any fetish I wouldn't have if you're involved."

"I don't know. There are some pretty icky ones out there. You should see some of the porn Josie watches. Gross."

"Well, if she ever breaks up with Candace, we'll have to set her up with Dennis. He can be freaky, too."

"I can hear you guys," he called from the living room.

"Go to sleep, Dennis," Jimmy retorted with a laugh.

"What kind of freaky?"

"I'll tell you later. Remind me to tell you the story about the watermelon at the picnic."

"Yep. Can still hear you. And don't you dare tell her that story."

I laughed and sighed in contentment. I was even half-tempted to cancel my date with Chief. I'd mentioned it to Jimmy earlier and he swatted me. Right on the ass.

I rubbed my hand over his belly, the taut muscles playing beneath my fingers. I couldn't even imagine how many sit-ups he must do in a day. Especially with all the beer he drank. I slid my hand down his thigh and back up his stomach, slipping under his T-shirt. He wasn't hairless, but he wasn't hairy, either. I could feel it, but it didn't grow in thick patches. Not even lower. His back and his butt were *completely* bare.

He must have been enjoying the tummy rubs. With my head on his chest, it was easy to notice the change in his breathing. The front of his sweatpants began moving, too.

I slipped my hand lower, tugging the knot at the waistband. Thankfully it wasn't done in some funky fireman knot. It pulled apart just like the ties on a shoe. I let go and lightly scratched my fingernails over the skin just above. His hips curled just a tiny bit. I'd found his sweet spot.

I put my palm back on his belly and started rubbing in circles again, moving lower each time, my fingers sliding under the elastic of his pants. Eventually, they found their way into the denser hair above his cock. I stopped moving and ran my fingers through it, gently stroking. His breathing sped up a bit more and so did the throbbing in his shaft. He'd grown hard as steel.

"That's fucking hot."

"What?" He had trouble speaking

"How hard you get when I play with you."

"Do you think it's hot that I'm hard, or do you think it's hot that you turn me on so much?"

"Little bit of both."

I pulled my hand out for a moment and lifted his shirt up enough I could rest my head on his bare skin. His nipple was right by my mouth. I slipped my hand back into his pants and gripped his flesh, running my hand down the length of it and squeezing the tip gently as I reached out with my tongue and licked his nipple. His hips bucked, and his arm pulled me against him tighter.

"Somebody likes that," I whispered, pulling his nipple into my mouth and gripping it with my teeth while flicking my tongue across it.

I didn't even have to move my hand, just hold him. His hips had found their own rhythm and he was fucking my hand. He lifted his knees and put his feet flat on the bed, angling his cock even higher.

I let go of his nipple with my mouth and scooted my head closer to the action. His hips stopped. I guess he didn't want to poke me in the face with it. Yet.

I trailed kisses all the way down, still holding him with my hand. Putting my ear against his lower abdomen, I brought his cock to my mouth. I held it as I licked the tip. His groan became music to my ears. Kissing the head, I gently sucked the tiniest bit of him into my mouth, rubbing my tongue against him as I did. His hand found the back of my head. He didn't push me further into his mouth, but his fingertips danced across the back of my scalp, massaging me. The other hand ran across my ass.

"Scoot closer," he breathed heavily, unable to reach his intended target.

I didn't want my leggings a sodden mess, so I sat up, sliding them off and onto the floor. I looked over my shoulder at him and winked.

I leaned back against him and slowly lifted my shirt up and over me, leaving me completely naked.

"Holy fuck."

I rolled back onto my side and sucked him into my mouth and scooted my ass closer to him. He was pulsing as I gripped him and began bobbing my head and hand in synchronous rhythm.

His hand ran over my ass again, but this time his middle finger slipped between the lips of my pussy, not in, but through. I gasped with him in my mouth as his finger slid smoothly across my clit. I could feel my wetness sliding slowly down over the crease of skin between leg and cheek. He was going to have to wash his sheets if he kept it up.

Then he twisted his torso, planting a gentle kiss on the part of my ass he could reach before dragging his teeth across it and biting down gently. I spread my legs and he cupped me, my heat planted firmly against the palm of his hand. I nearly squealed when he began rubbing. I wanted more.

I pulled my ass away and rolled onto my stomach, never taking him from my mouth. Getting my knees under me, I carefully lifted one over him, lying down on his chest, my pussy nearly in his face. As I sucked him harder and pumped his flesh, he leaned in and licked me from clit to ass, parting my lips and diving inside. My hips refused to obey me and found a will of their own, grinding me against his mouth, tongue, and chin.

I tried concentrating on sucking his dick. I didn't know how much more I could take, and I wanted him to come. My thoughts became obliterated when he shoved his tongue inside me. He didn't stop there. He began pushing it in and out, matching my rhythm. I closed my eyes and relaxed, taking him as much into my mouth as I could. I felt the tip slip into the back of my throat, but it didn't bother me as I concentrated on breathing slowly through my nose.

I could feel every muscle in his body tense as he began frantically tapping me on my ass, unable to speak. I knew what he wanted to tell me. I forced him in a little further as my orgasm washed over me.

He exploded straight into my throat, I could feel the heat as it slid down. It wasn't a bad experience and didn't leave a taste in my mouth. I pulled back as my hips began frantically lifting me off his tongue, riding wave after wave of pleasure. I cried out and buried my face next to his still throbbing shaft.

I sighed and panted, trying to get the room to stop spinning, until finally I rolled off him, propping my legs up on the wall above his bed.

"I need a cigarette," I said exasperatedly.

"Do you smoke?"

"No. But fuck, that deserves something."

"I can still hear you," Dennis called from the other room.

The heat rushed from my body and collected in my cheeks. My blush threatening to end my existence. Jimmy started chuckling.

"Well, you should have just come watched then," I said, trying to diffuse the situation.

Jimmy slapped my thigh with another chuckle. "Don't tell him that, he probably would."

The thought didn't scare me like it should have...

Chapter 23

"So, what did you do today."

I felt the blush crawl up my cheeks but answered anyway. "Had breakfast with the girls, got my appliances ordered, and put the deposit down and signed the contract for the bookstore renovations."

"Wow, look at you go." Chief managed to sound moderately impressed. We were riding in his Jeep, on our way to dinner. I didn't really make him drive us all the way to Syracuse, either. I was way too hungry for that. He seemed both relieved and disappointed at the same time when I let him off the hook.

"Oh, and I went to see Jimmy. He's home from the hospital."

"I know, he called to let me know. I told him and Dennis to stick together and about the two-man team plan."

I briefly wondered what *else* they talked about. The men in my life had a tendency to overshare and didn't think twice about it. It had almost reached creepy proportions. "Good. I did too while I was there, but maybe they'll listen to you more than me."

"I doubt it. They respect you, more than you think."

"Yeah, right."

"Oh, shush. You know they do."

I let it go. The only person who respected me was Josie and only when I was pissed off.

"So. What's for dinner?"

"Do you like steak?"

"Only more than sex..." I realized I probably shouldn't have said that. For so many reasons. Technically Jimmy and I hadn't exactly *had* sex, but I'm sure that was the first thought that popped into Chief's head.

"Then I'm taking you to the right place. The porterhouse will blow your...mind."

I could see how this night was going to go.

"Great."

He chuckled softly. I wanted to punch him.

We were on the outskirts of town. He pulled into a semi-crowded parking lot next to what looked like, for lack of a better description, a giant log cabin. The sign out front glowed brightly in the crisp evening air and had a blue ox emblazoned across it.

"Bunyan's?"

"Yep. Friend of mine named Paul opened it up a few years back."

"Are you kidding me right now? You have a friend named Paul Bunyan?"

"No. I have a friend named *Paul* who opened a restaurant called *Bunyan's*."

"Oh. Okay then." I didn't know how to feel about that.

"They do serve an ox steak though..."

"Shut up." I got out of the car laughing.

We walked through a little bit of crunchy snow to get to the front door. He opened it and let me get in out of the cold. I stamped my feet on the thick rubber backed mat in front of the door and slipped out of my leather jacket. Chief took it from me and hung it from the rack by the entrance.

"Thanks."

"My pleasure."

"Hey, folks. How many?"

"Two, please," he said to the hostess.

She blushed a little and grabbed two thick menus from the stack by the podium. "Right this way."

The inside of the restaurant was even more rustic than the outside. If that were even possible. Kind of Cracker Barrell meets hunting lodge. Antlers were everywhere. The center of the place was dominated by a deer antler chandelier hanging from the apex of the vaulted roof.

"Wow."

"Don't let their suave décor fool you. They serve a pretty good piece of meat."

I refrained from making the joke I wanted to make and followed the hostess quietly. She led us to a quiet booth in the back by the window. It had started snowing again, glistening brightly as it fell past the light affixed to the outside wall. With the candle on the table, the effect was quite cozy.

I sat against the back wall and Chief sat down in front of me. "Kelly will be with you shortly," the hostess said cheerily and handed us our menus.

Chief set his down on the table without looking at it. "Know what you want?" I asked.

"I'm thinking prime rib. Twenty-ounce. With a loaded baked potato and glazed baby carrots."

"Wow. Come here much?"

"Once or twice."

"A week?"

"Maybe."

I chuckled and opened up the menu. "The porterhouse, huh?"

"It's their best steak. The prime rib is delicious. So is the filet. Depends on what kind of meat you like."

I refused to take the bait. Again. He was making it too easy. And I didn't think he was doing it on purpose…

"I like all of them, but I'll take your suggestion."

"Good evening. Can I start you guys out with some beverages?"

"I'll have a glass of pinot please." I wanted wine.

"Bud."

"Did you need a few minutes to look at the menu?"

"I think we're ready to order."

"For you, miss?"

"Porterhouse, medium rare, baked potato with butter, and a side of mushrooms."

"Sir?"

"I was going to order the prime rib, but I think I'll have what she's having. Load the potato, though."

"You got it."

She headed to put in our order. "Change your mind?"

"Yeah. That sounded delicious."

I smiled and held out my hand. Curious, he took it. I just held his hand from across the table. It felt like something one would do on a date, and that's what this was supposed to be. He visibly relaxed.

"Going to be honest. This is the first time I've done this in a really long while. If I make a fool of myself, please forgive me."

"You miss her, don't you?"

"Every damn day."

"Sorry, Bill."

"It's okay. It's in the past."

I nodded, rubbing the palm of his hand with the tips of my fingers. I felt like a change of topic was needed. "Josie and Candace actually came up with a plan."

"Is it safe?"

"And a shortcut. Holding a coven meeting and interviewing everyone at once."

"In the same room?"

"That would be up to you. You're the expert. But at least we can get it knocked out in a short amount of time."

"Might not be a bad idea. Where?"

"My house?"

"Killer already knows where you live. Maybe a return visit will bring out their guilt."

"We can call it a potluck dinner."

"You really want a killer bringing food. Poisoned potatoes…"

"Okay. I'll have it catered." I laughed. He made a good point.

"This Sunday. Tomorrow is too soon."

"I'll call everyone. See what their schedules are like and see if they can switch shifts if needed."

"Good. Maybe we'll actually get somewhere. I'm tired of reacting and people getting hurt."

"Me, too."

Kelly returned with our drinks. She set my wine down in front of me and the bottle in front of Chief. "Glass?"

He shook his head. "Bottle is fine."

"I'll be back with your food in a little bit. You need anything else?"

"No, thanks."

I watched her walk away. She seemed kind of young to be working at a steak restaurant, but she was nice and sweet. "Good job for a kid."

"She's new. Or at least I've never seen her in here in the once or twice times I've been here this week." He grinned.

"Maybe she's a witch and older than both of us."

"That would be funny. I often wonder if there are other witches around that we don't know about. One's that don't find the coven. It's not like we walk around with 'I'm a Witch' T-shirts on. I'm surprised we have as many in our coven as we do."

"Like finds like. Mysterious forces and all that. I can't even begin to tell you how many times witches showed up at our doorstep, people not from our town."

"Yeah. I can imagine. It's how Candace found us. And the two married couples we have. None of them are from Cedar Falls. The rest of us grew up here."

"I asked Candace straight out if she were the killer. Just joking, of course. She answered right away. I thought Josie was going to scorch me."

"She's an interesting young lady. Don't think she'd be capable of hurting a fly. You should see her around animals."

"I can picture that. You know she's fae-blooded, right?"

"Not for certain, but I kind of figured."

"I asked her that, too. She came right out and said yes but didn't elaborate. Then she got misty eyed when we told her we didn't care."

"Some witches do. Some witches would want to use her blood for all sorts of dark and twisted stuff."

"Yeah. Poor girl. I told her she was stuck with us until this was over. She didn't seem to mind."

"Good."

He paused a moment and took the opportunity to lift my hand up. The table was narrow enough that he brought the back of my hand to his lips and planted a gentle kiss.

"What was that for?"

"I've been wanting to do that all night. You look absolutely amazing this evening. Well, most evenings, but particularly tonight."

He wasn't a smooth talker, so I knew the compliment was from his heart. It warmed me up a little and made me break out in a goofy smile. He had that effect on me. Subtle warm charm. "Thank you. You look very handsome yourself."

He chuckled and sat back in the booth. "Sure."

"Don't be a dork. You got all the women folk of Cedar Falls drooling over you."

"Yeah, right."

"What is it with guys? Either they think they *are* the shit when they're not. Or they think they're shit when they're not. You are rugged, masculine, fine, and handsome. Any girl would count themselves lucky to be with you."

"Even you?"

"Yes."

That hadn't been the answer he was expecting. He almost choked on his beer. "Here I thought I wore you down with my witty repartee and you *deigned* to have a date with me out of pity."

"*Far* from it. I'll admit, you can be quite annoying, but then again, I probably bring out those qualities in you."

"This is true. I'm a much nicer person when you're not around." He winked to let me know he was joking.

"I don't doubt it. I'm a frustrating piece of work."

"But I wouldn't change one damn thing about you. You're fun. Beautiful. Sexy. And to be honest, quite perfect."

And here I'd just been thinking he wasn't a smooth talker...

"Here we go," Kelly said as she brought our food. She set my plate down in front of me. "Butter only on the potato." And then she set Chief's down in front of him. "And a loaded one for you. Want me to get you some more drinks?"

"Yes, please."

"I'll have one more glass, too."

"Be right back."

I put my cloth napkin on my lap and grabbed the steak knife and fork off the table. I cut the tip off the steak and popped it in my mouth. Chief had paused to watch my reaction. The steak almost melted on my tongue like butter. I hardly even had to chew.

"Oh, my Lady."

"Told you."

"Shut up and eat."

It didn't take long to polish off the food and the second round of beverages. I was full, sleepy, and wanted nothing more than to curl up on something.

Chief paid cash for everything and I noticed he left a *very* generous tip for our waitress. "And everybody yells at me for throwing my money around."

"Not only was the meal perfect, but so was her service. She made the first date I've been on in years very memorable. I probably should have doubled it and thanked her personally."

"Wow. That was a *very* sweet sentiment."

He shrugged. "That also happened to be true. Thank you, Dot. For going out with a lonely old man and brightening his life lately."

We were standing outside the restaurant in the falling snow, but I didn't care. I slid my arms around him under his open jacket and pressed myself against him. Stepping up on my toes, I kissed him.

It turned into something hot enough to melt the snow around us. I could feel myself melting like the steak I ate. Pulling him tighter, I ran my hand down his ass. I groaned in appreciation while kissing him.

A car pulling out of the parking lot honked at us and the guy gave us a thumbs up out the window. We broke our kiss, laughing. The way every kiss should end.

"Wow."

I nodded. He had summed it up perfectly.

"Would you mind doing this again sometime?"

"Sure. But I'm buying."

"We'll arm wrestle for it."

"Oh, Chief. There are *so* many more interesting forms of wrestling. Let me pick…"

He laughed and let me go, snagging my hand as we walked to the car. "Come on, let's go."

"Where we going?"

"Where do you want to go? Don't feel bad if it's home. I'm sure you've had a long day, and you did promise me another date."

If I wasn't as full as I was, I probably would have volunteered to go to a bar or something. But vegging out on my couch or my bed sounded very wonderful. "Home, but if you would like to come in and watch a movie or just relax, I would be fine with that, too."

"Okay."

He squeezed my hand and opened the car door for me. "Such a gentleman," I teased and got into the Jeep.

Chapter 24

"What time is it?"

I vaguely listened as he shuffled around and grabbed my phone from the nightstand, handing it to me. I blinked and stared at the screen. It was almost nine in the morning. I'd set my alarm for some damn reason and couldn't remember why. I shut it off and tossed it on the bed to the other side of Chief.

Chief?

I blinked and lifted my head. Sure enough, he was under my comforter and I'd been sleeping in the crook of his arm. I groaned and tried to remember what had happened last night.

Memories of getting home, watching a movie, and drinking flittered through my brain. I remember him being too drunk to drive home and me offering my bed. I sighed in relief as I remember crawling in next to him and nothing happening. We had both passed out.

"How's your head?" He asked softly.

"Throbbing. Text Josie to bring us water and aspirin." I really wanted aspirin.

"We should probably get dressed first."

I lifted the comforter up and saw we were both naked. No wonder I was having such happy little dreams. I had his leg trapped between mine...

My eyes widened as I saw his morning wood.

"Maybe we should wait for that to evaporate."

"Not my fault. I'm in bed with a beautiful naked woman. I don't think it's going to evaporate any time soon."

I couldn't resist. I reached out and pushed it down. It sprang right back up. "Wow." Not only did I act like a teenager, I giggled like one, too.

"That's not helping either."

"I'd um, take care of for you, but I don't know how I'd feel about that."

"I know."

"Do you?" I turned my head to look him in the eye, but they were still closed. He did have a goofy smile plastered on his lips, though.

"Yes, Dot. I do. You're dating Jimmy. You're dating me. I'm guessing you and Jimmy have done more than sleep next to each other and you're wondering if I'm okay with that."

"Well, not to put it bluntly, but yes."

"The answer is, kind of."

"Kind of?"

"Do I know, yes. Do I want to picture it in my head? No. But I'm not jealous of him or anything. You are you. You date and do whatever you want with whomever you want. I don't own you. If anything, it's the other way around. I was married for a very long time. My wife passed away. Do I want to get married again? No. Do I want to live with anybody? No. Do I want to keep dating you, do I want to do stuff like this again, do I want to take our relationship further? Yes. But, again, that is up to you. You are the high priestess of our coven. We are yours. Or, at least Jimmy and I are…"

"Call me old fashioned, but that outlook is…different from most men. Yet it seems to be the common thought between all of you. My mother never married. She's had multiple lovers at the same time. I thought that wasn't normal. Mostly because it was my mother. Am I the weird one?"

"Definitely," he said and laughed.

"I walked into that one."

"Yep. But, if you want my honest thoughts on the matter, I think it might be some sort of genetic disposition inherent to witches. Kind of like a queen bee. *Everyone* flirted with Becca. She wasn't interested, but that never stopped them. I don't know. Maybe it's a pheromone or something. It's not like any scientific research has been done on witches since the middle ages."

I shrugged and put my hand on his stomach. His logic was kind of sound. My fingers danced across his skin while I thought about it. As I did, the contrast between him and Jimmy became quite apparent. He wasn't as muscular as Jimmy, but he didn't have an ounce of fat on him. He had more stomach and chest hair, too. I kind of liked it.

Chief shifted a little and lifted his arm, pulling me a little closer. He kissed the top of my head and I rubbed my cheek against him. His leg slid further up between mine and I felt him against me. I didn't think that he'd done it on purpose, but it felt good. His warmth and the muscles in his thigh creating just enough pressure.

"Your leg's not falling asleep, is it?"

"No?"

"Your arm?"

"No. I'm quite comfortable. Except for my pounding head."

I kissed his chest and settled down. "I don't want to get up."

"Me, neither."

"Um. You already are."

"You're funny."

I chuckled into his skin. He smelled really good. Even first thing in the morning. I sighed and stretched, digging his leg in a little more.

Ooh.

Experimentally, I stretched my back and the feeling between my legs intensified. I caught myself breathing a little heavier. I brought my hand down lazily over the comforter and back up, trapping him between my forearm and his stomach. I could feel him throbbing beneath it.

Fuck. Now I'm hot.

I began grinding my hips a little, slowly at first. The friction sending shuddering chills up my spine.

"You okay?"

"Yes. Just doing some morning stretches."

"Oh. Cuz it felt like you were grinding against my thigh."

"That, too. Is that okay?"

"Yes."

"Sorry, taking things slowly, but really turned on right now."

"Shucky darns."

I let go of the pretenses and slid myself up and down his thigh as far as my hips would go. I moved closer to him and put my face in the crook of his neck. I'm sure my shallow breathing in his ear wasn't something he'd been expecting.

"I'm going to be honest. This is hot." His voice rumbled in his chest, exciting me further.

I could feel him shifting, rubbing himself against the underside my arm. "If I asked you to, would you touch yourself for me?"

"If you asked, there isn't much I *wouldn't* do."

I could feel my wetness spreading between us, making his leg that much slipperier. I was in heaven. I grabbed the comforter and peeled it back, his cock springing into the air. It was definitely the largest one I'd ever seen. I didn't even know they *got* that big. I wanted to touch it, feel it, but I wasn't ready. "Do it," I whispered into his ear, kissing the lobe.

He reached down and curled his fist around the base, slowly stroking upward and over the tip. The journey took a while. He bucked his hips as he did it. "This isn't going to take long," he warned.

I pulled his hand away and brought it to my mouth. I moistened my lips and dragged my tongue across his palm, moistening it before placing it back. He groaned as he stroked himself again.

"Dot…"

"Do it, Bill. I want to see you come."

I pressed my cheek against his and watched the show from his perspective, grinding myself hard against his rigid thigh. I pressed myself against him, letting his flesh drive me apart and across my more sensitive spots,

"Fuck," I breathed out, doubling my efforts.

He groaned next to me.

I pulled my hand back from under the covers, letting go of some of my inhibitions. I grabbed the base of his cock and stroked him, too. As his hand slid down, mine came up to meet his.

"I'm going to come."

"Do it. Let me see."

I felt my orgasm building. I wanted, *needed*, to time it perfectly. His hips curled hard and his breathing stopped. He shuddered from his torso to his toes. It drove his leg *hard* against my aching pussy and it flooded me with an orgasm I hadn't been expecting. My toes curled, and I felt the scream building in my throat at the exact moment his semen burst forth from his cock in a spray worthy of a dirty movie.

The scream that had been building in my throat tore free as waves and waves of ecstasy spread from my groin and every muscle in my body. My bucking hips slowed, and I collapsed next to him, panting.

My door burst open and Josie stood there wielding a kitchen knife, Candace standing behind and peeking around her, hands poised to cast magic.

"Oh, fuck me," she said and rolled her eyes, closing the door.

"Oops," I said after she left.

"Um… Yeah. That was an interesting way to wake up."

"That was fucking hot," I said referring to our play, not being barged in on by my roommate.

I rolled back against him, staring at the pool of semen on his stomach. I touched it tentatively with the tip of my finger, dragging it around and playing with it. I couldn't even imagine that amount being shot into my mouth. I'd have choked to death.

"Don't you masturbate?"

"Um… Yes?"

"How long ago?"

"In the shower before our date."

"Holy fuck."

"What?"

"Nothing. That's just… That's a lot of come. Not going to lie."

"Thanks?"

"You're welcome."

"I need a towel."

"Me, too."

∞ ∞ ∞

"I'll see you later, but I'll call you and let you know as soon as possible about the coven meeting tomorrow."

"I'll talk to Herb today about possibly catering."

"Good luck. He hates catering."

"Ugh. That sucks. I'll beg if I have to."

"That might work."

"Bye, Chief."

"Bye, Dot." He leaned down and kissed me gently on the lips before heading out. I sighed and smiled at his retreating back before softly closing the front door.

I turned around to face an angry looking Josie and an amused looking Candace hiding behind her.

"What?"

"No more sexy screams until the killer is caught! I thought it turned out to be Chief and he was killing you in your bedroom. Damnit, Dot. You gave me a fucking heart attack."

"I'm sorry," I said with a chuckle and stepped forward to give her a hug. She held up her hand to stop me.

"Shower first."

I started laughing. Surprisingly, Candace did, too. "He didn't get any on me. It all landed on him."

Her face was worth the embarrassment.

"Okay, now that that discussion is over, we can move on to the next topic of importance."

"What?" I asked warily.

"That monster he's been hiding in them blue jeans. Holy shit, Dot! He could play baseball with that thing!" She started giggling like a school girl.

"I know, right? That's gonna hurt. But probably in a good way."

"You haven't yet?" She made a childish gesture with her fingers.

"No. Jimmy and I haven't technically, either."

"So, which one you gonna do first?"

Our conversation had moved into the living room and we sat down to gossip like we always do.

"Honestly, I don't know. I like them both. A lot. I'll probably just play it by ear. Or other parts."

Josie grinned at me.

"Do they both know?" Candace's honesty never ceased to catch me off guard.

I nodded emphatically. "Yes. I would never do anything like that behind their backs."

The smile found its way back on her face. "Good. Then enjoy it. It never ends well when others find out secrets that shouldn't have been secrets."

"What do you mean?"

"Some of our coven pledged faithfulness to each other. Some lusted for others, some succumbed to that lust. It has poisoned their hearts..."

Marge's voice repeated in my head, "The two boys I saw with the same woman, but Rebecca was always with the chief."

"Candace, are you referring to Richie and Dane?"

She shook her head. "They were part of it, but not the ones that succumbed."

"Who?"

"I shouldn't say. It is not my secret to share."

"Would you humor me? This falls in line with something someone said to me the other day. That she had seen both of them with the same woman. Is that who you are talking about?"

"Yes."

"This person was married? She had pledged her faithfulness and broke it?"

She nodded, surprised at my words.

"Candace this might be a big missing piece of the puzzle and help us stop the killings. Would you tell me who the woman is?"

She thought about it before nodding. "Yes. If it is that important, I'll tell you. It was Cindy."

"Cindy Connors?"

"Yes. She had relations with a few members of the coven."

"More than those two?"

She nodded. It was like trying to get information out of a teenager. I forced myself to be patient with her. "Who else?"

"Jimmy and Dennis."

Rage and jealousy reared their ugly little heads. I found myself clenching my fists and then realized I was being a hypocritical little bitch. I didn't know where it had come from, but my entire being screamed, "Mine," as soon as

Jimmy's name left her lips. I'd have to explore that further. Later.

I looked at Josie. "Call the chief. Tell him to check on Jimmy and Dennis and tell him they might be in danger. I'll fill him in later."

She got up from the couch and ran to her bedroom, leaving Candace and I alone.

Before I questioned her further, I thought about the information she had already given me. It wasn't adding up. I sat back on the love seat and thought about it. The person who shot at Jimmy was a guy. Or, at least Jimmy *thought* it was a guy. Cindy Connors was *very* feminine though. Even in a jacket and a ski mask, nobody would mistake her for a man.

Blake?

That made a little more sense. Jealousy can be a bitch, as I just experienced first-hand.

But where did I fall into it? And the chief's wife?

Candace looked very uncomfortable sitting there while I gathered my thoughts. She was practically squirming in her seat. "I'm sorry! I was just thinking about what you told me."

"I thought you were mad…"

"No, no. I'm sorry, sweetie."

She visibly relaxed and she shifted her hands under her to stop fidgeting. "Just trying to figure out how I and the chief's wife fit in with the Connors."

"The chief's wife was the object of lust."

"Pardon?"

"Blake would leer at her all the time. I heard him talking to her more than once about how he wanted her. It was kind of disgusting. At least Becca thought so. She made it plain as day that she would never want him. It made Blake angry."

"People say a lot in front of you, don't they?"

"I'm small and blend in. Most of the time people don't notice me."

"And yet you're a nurse?"

"Pediatric nurse. Kids like me."

Well the mystery of the step stools was solved. The murders, however, were not. "I still don't get why I was targeted?"

She shrugged her shoulders. "I shared what I knew."

I stood up and walked over to her, kneeling in front of her. "That is more information than *anybody* else has provided to me. Thank you."

"You're welcome," she said with a little blush.

Again, the feeling that she was hiding something horrible in her past washed over me. It wasn't a feeling that she'd done something bad, but that someone had hurt her *very, very* badly. "Are you okay, Candace?"

She looked at me confusedly. "Yes?"

"Just a feeling I get when I talk to you. That someone hurt you."

Her eyes went wide and she looked to be eight-milliseconds from a panic attack. I put my hand on her head. "You don't have to tell me. Ever. I'd never ask, but if you ever *do* need to talk about it, you know you can always come to me, okay?"

She calmed almost immediately and gave me a grateful nod. I opened my arms inviting her in for hug instead of just hugging her. She nodded and smiled, closing the distance between us.

I even planted a small kiss on her head. She smelled like flowers and rain. I could see why Josie would be attracted to her. Hell, I was straight and a *little* attracted to her.

I let go and she slid back on the couch.

"Thanks for your help. I'm going to go see if I can figure out what it all means. You're the best, Candace."

Chapter 25

My phone rang just as I was getting into the car. I'd thrown on some clothes, brushed my teeth, and downed a few aspirin and bottles of water. I'd dialed Jimmy a few times and Chief once. No one had answered.

I looked down at my screen and saw Jimmy's number. "About damn time. You okay?"

"Yes? Why wouldn't I be?"

"Might have figured out who the killer is..."

"Who?"

"Blake Connors."

After a few moments of silence, I stared back down at the phone to make sure the call hadn't dropped. It hadn't. The timer was still going. I put it back up to my ear.

"You still there?"

"Yeah."

"You okay?"

"Depends. Do you think less of me?"

"Whoa there, Sheriff. That was before I ambled into to town. Right?"

"Yes."

"No, I don't think less of you. She might have been a married woman, but it was her who broke her vows. Not you."

"Oh, thank the Lady. I thought you would have been mad."

"Don't even go there. What about Dennis. Is he there with you?"

"Yeah."

"Okay. Stay together. I'm going to find Chief and figure out what's going on. Did he call you?"

"I just woke up. Ten missed calls from him and three from you. I'll call him after I hang up."

"Okay."

"Call me later."

"I will."

"Dot..."

"What?"

"Stay safe."

I knew that wasn't what he was going to say, but I let it go. "You, too."

I started up the car and backed it out of the driveway, heading into town. The Chief would either be at the station or the diner.

I drove slowly past the diner but didn't see him inside. His Jeep was, however, parked in front of the station. I pulled into the lot between it and the bookstore, parking closer to the station. The bookstore was currently under demolition and a good portion of the spots were currently occupied by a large dumpster.

Parking, I shut off the car and headed around the corner. Chief was exiting the building at the same time and we almost collided. "Dot?"

"Were you expecting someone else?"

"I just got off the phone with Jimmy."

"Yeah. I talked to him, finally."

"Got time to talk?"

"Bet your ass. How come you didn't answer?"

"I was doing some investigating. You know. Like cops do."

"Sorry."

"Don't be. I had just finished when Jimmy called. I hung up with him and you showed up."

"I should have known. I'm just worried."

He pulled me into a quick hug and gave me a kiss on my forehead. "I know. I should have called you sooner. I'm the one who is sorry. After Josie called..."

"Yeah. I can't believe we didn't put two and two together sooner."

"Come on. I'll buy you a coffee."

"I'll buy. I want food."

"How do you not weigh six-hundred pounds?"

"How are you still alive after asking horrible questions like that to women?"

"My subtle charm."

"Good luck with that."

He opened the door for me at least. I slipped into the diner, waving to Marge.

She came shuffling over. "Morning, you two. Breakfast or lunch?"

"Breakfast."

"Lunch," Chief answered.

"You need menus?"

At least we both said, "No."

"Sit down. I'll bring your drinks."

Chief started heading to the counter, where he normally sat. I stood where I was and coughed at him. He stopped and turned around, confusion clearly etched upon his face. I pointed at my usual table. He rolled his eyes and sat in the booth.

"So, let me get this straight. You think it's Cindy Connors?"

I shook my head. "No. I think it's Blake. Cindy wasn't faithful, and she slept with Dane, Richie, Jimmy, *and* Dennis. I think Blake found out about it and got more than a little pissed off."

"But what about you? And what about Becca?"

"I think Becca might have been..." I didn't want to continue. I didn't think Chief knew about Blake's crush on her. His leering glances and whispered overtures. "Blake had a thing for Rebecca. Candace saw him always staring at her and he even propositioned her more than once. In a not so endearing way, I might add."

"I know about those. She told me every time. When I questioned him, I got a bit physical and he filed a complaint, so I had to back off. If he wanted her so bad, why kill her?"

"Maybe because he couldn't have her? Maybe because she kept rejecting him?"

"Maybe. I'm not going to lie, though. I beat the shit out of him. I didn't get the feeling he did it, though. And that doesn't explain you. Why blow up your car and show up at your house with a gun?"

"I have no idea."

"Maybe Jimmy *was* his target with the gun. His truck was parked in front of your house."

"But what about blowing up my car?"

"That I can't figure out. The rest of the logic is sound, though. Glad I never slept with Cindy."

Marge showed up with a coffee and coke for me and coffee for Chief. "What you having to eat?"

"I'll have a burger, well, with fries."

She jotted it down and looked at me.

"Double stack of pancakes."

"No omelet?"

"No, but I'll have a side of bacon."

"Sure thing, kids. Have it out shortly."

I smiled at her retreating back. It would be a sad day in Cedar Falls when Marge wouldn't be able to wait tables anymore. I'd just gotten into town and couldn't imagine it without her. Or Herb.

"I was running a check to see if the Connors own any firearms. As soon as I hear back, I'll match the caliber to the bullets you pulled out of Jimmy. We can get a warrant if it matches. You still up for the little soiree?"

"Thinking you can get some information out of him?"

"I'm going to try."

"So, I should talk to Herb then, huh?"

"Good luck. As I said."

"Just you watch."

"Hey, Marge, tell Herb I wanna talk to him when he has a moment."

"Sure thing, Dot. Herb! Next break, go see Dot," she called through the open kitchen window.

I saw him wiggle his head and look around the dining room. He waved when he saw me. "Okay!"

"What are you doing tonight?"

"Quiet evening at home. Bottle of wine. Maybe a nice bath."

"Alone?"

"No. Josie and Candace are there."

"I meant the bath."

"I know. It's just more fun to tease you."

He sighed and sipped his coffee. "Pain in the ass."

"What was that?"

"I said I like your ass."

"Good answer. What are you doing tonight?"

"I think I might be keeping an eye on the Connors... Was seeing how you felt about a stakeout."

"Will there be donuts and coffee?"

"There can be."

"Then I'm in. Pick me up whenever."

"I don't want to interrupt your bath."

"I wasn't really going to take one. I'm more of a shower kind of girl. I just wanted you to picture me in a tub of water, completely naked."

"I was."

"Then my mission was a success."

He chuckled. "I had a lot of fun last night. And this morning."

The rat bastard made me blush. Just when I was getting the upper hand. "You suck."

"Do you?"

"I do. I'm not an expert by any stretch of the imagination…"

"That makes me happy."

"One of those, no experience necessary, kinda things. Huh?"

"Yes." He smiled and took another sip of coffee.

"Is there such a thing as a bad blowjob?"

He nodded emphatically and winced. "Hell yes."

I couldn't help it. I laughed. I could see the pain in his eyes. He was speaking from experience. "Were teeth involved?"

"Yes."

"Ouch."

"You have no idea."

"Yeah, I do. Not every guy is a natural with their mouth either."

"Touché."

"Funny you say that, because some guys think they are fencing when they do it."

I'd finally done it. Coffee came out of Chief's nose. Score was oh to one in my favor. "Can you not say shit like that when I'm drinking?"

"Oops."

Herb himself brought out our food and set it down in front of us. He pulled up a chair from the table next to us and sat down at the end of the booth.

"What's up? More properties you want to look at?"

"Not yet. I'm having a party at my house for special friends of ours." I narrowed my eyes hoping he would catch my drift. "I know it's last minute, but would you consider catering? My appliances are toast and the new ones won't get delivered until sometime next week."

He sighed heavily. "I absolutely abhor catering. If it's for you, I'll do it, though. What were you thinking?"

"Couple pans of spaghetti and sauce. Salad. Maybe some garlic bread? Keep it easy and surprise me."

"How about some chicken parm to go along with it?"

"Oh, that's a good idea. Yes, please. Maybe some meatballs or Italian sausage, too?"

"I'll see what I can whip up. You want me to let you know how much or just bill you?"

"Bill me. And add ten percent for the short notice."

"I will do no such thing."

I sighed. The people in Cedar Falls could be so difficult. "Fine. I'll just give Marge an extra big tip, you big dolt."

He chortled. "That I can live with. What time you want me to deliver?"

"You deliver?"

"Not me personally. I have a kid who makes deliveries for me on special occasions."

"What special occasions?"

He sighed. "Holidays mostly. There are a lot of families in town that can't afford holiday meals. Don't spread it around, but Marge and I cook for those since it's just the two of us. We never had any kids and so we try to do nice things for people."

The tears were streaming down my face and getting my pancakes a little soggy. I poured some syrup on them and tried to get my shit together. Chief handed me a napkin. "Damn it, Herb."

"What?"

"I'm promoting you to Saint Herb. Change your nametag."

He chuckled softly. "Don't let Marge hear you say that. She'll give you a list a mile long of all my disqualifications."

"Would you two do me the honor of having Christmas dinner with me at my home this year? You've both made me feel like part of this town the moment I walked through your door."

"I'd absolutely adore that, but we have so many people counting on us every year, it's become almost a tradition."

"I wasn't expecting you to. Josie and I, and maybe a few of the boys are going to come help you this year. We're going to get those meals prepped, cooked, and delivered a little faster. *Then* we're going to go relax at my house, have dinner, drink lots, and open presents. Would that be okay?"

It was his turn to wipe his eyes. Bill handed him a napkin. "That would be...great." He managed to get the words out with a minimal amount of cracking in his voice.

"In addition, you will have an invoice for the food you are prepping ready for me upon my arrival. And don't say shit. Keep it shut, Herb. This is my Yule– I mean this is my Christmas present to you and Marge. You've been doing this for how many years? I don't want to hear a peep out of you."

He just nodded. I could hear the sniffles and see him struggling to fight back the tears. I knew the symptoms because I had the same ones.

"Dot. I can't even..."

"Then don't. Just shush and nod your head."

"Okay."

"Tell the delivery guy to have it to my house around four in the afternoon."

He nodded. "I should...uh...get back in the uh... kitchen." He wiped his eyes one more time and stuffed the napkin in his pocket. Standing, he slid the chair back to the table. Before he left, he leaned down and put his hand on my shoulder, kissing me on the top of my head. "Thank you, Dot."

"You're welcome," I said and grinned up at him. He headed back into the kitchen.

"I think you just got adopted." Chief was sitting back in the booth, not touching his food. He'd watched the whole exchange silently. At least *he* wasn't crying.

"Good. Because honestly, I wouldn't mind having a set of parents in town. They're good peoples."

"Dot... What you just did..."

"Too much?"

"No. I wish there were more people like you and them in this town. He wasn't kidding when he said there are a lot of people who have come to rely on him and Marge around the holidays. There's a ton of kids who go without a happy holiday. We do a toy drive at the station, but we rarely come up with much."

"Well. We'll do what we can this year. Next year... Next year is going to be different."

He just smiled and picked up his burger. "Can't save the whole town, Dot."

"Just you fucking watch me, Chief."

Chapter 26

"Why exactly are we doing this if they're coming to my house tomorrow?"

"Gut feeling. I think if it is Blake, the thought of being gathered with the coven might set him on edge. Maybe he'll do something stupid tonight, like try to get rid of a gun or finish off Jimmy."

"The officer is still watching his place?"

"The officer and Dwight and Jason. Not playing around with his safety, Dot. Don't worry."

I nodded and shivered in the Cherokee. We couldn't keep it running and it was fucking cold outside. Chief had a blanket draped over his lap. I had two, but half-expected the blankets to freeze stiff in the next twenty minutes or so. I was holding a mug of coffee in my hands just to keep them from shaking.

"Want to get into the back seat? I can sit with you and we can share body heat. Blankets, too."

"Chief, are you just trying to get me in the back seat to make out on our stakeout?"

His bark of laughter almost caused me to spill my coffee in my lap. "No. I'm sorry, but that was funny. You're a poet."

"No. My brain is just frozen." I set my coffee in the cup holder and stared at him.

"So yes, to the back seat?"

"Promise to behave?"

"Yes," he said slowly.

"Then no. I don't wanna." I grinned and opened my door, practically diving into the back seat. "Hurry up."

He got out and back in, sliding into the cold, leather seat. "That just froze my ass," he complained and spread his blanket over our laps. I put my two on top of it and bundled it up over our chests. For once in my life I was glad I wore a bra. I'd probably have sliced my arm open on my nipple by now if I hadn't.

While we waited for the air under the blankets to warm, my teeth started chattering. Chief had been staring at their empty driveway and stopped when he heard the sound. He reached over and laid me down on his lap, covering me with his arms. My head was the only thing above the blankets. His legs were cool, but warmer than I was. I rested my head back against his stomach, feeling horrible that he was above the blanket.

"That's enough of this shit. I don't care if they sense the magic or not. We're going to freeze to death. I'll keep it low." I closed my eyes and whispered, "*Coinnigh muid te.*"

A warm zephyr formed in the middle of the Jeep, slowly stirring the air inside. Quickly the chill left, leaving it a little warmer, but not too warm.

Chief closed his eyes. "I can't even feel it."

"It uses *minimal* power. Heating with convection instead of blaring heat."

"That's pretty handy. You'll have to teach me the incantation later. I could use one of those in my bedroom."

"That's what she said." I could be childish. I admit it.

"What?"

"I could use one… Never mind. She said joke."

He cast me a sidelong glance and looked back up at the driveway. This was going to be a long night.

I shifted on his lap. "Tell me a story."

"You suck at this whole stakeout thing."

"I didn't know it was going to be this boring."

He poked me in the side and then pointed out the windshield. "Maybe not."

I sat up slowly and saw a car backing out of the driveway. Luckily there was a street lamp overhead. Only one head was visible in the driver's seat. Whichever one it was, they were alone.

"We're going to follow them."

"What if it's Cindy and not Blake?"

"Could you see if it was a man or a woman?"

"No. Could you? Aren't you supposed to have binoculars or something?"

"They're in the front seat."

"Shit."

"Get in the front. We'll follow the car."

"Okay."

We did, and he started it up, but didn't turn on the headlights until the car turned onto Main. He flipped the headlights on and made the turn, following at a very respectable distance.

I realized where we were heading…

"Chief."

"I know."

I texted Josie and told her to get out of the house, through the back door if possible. She texted back an okay. That was a load off my mind.

The car stopped on the curb of the street a few houses down. Chief pulled into the closest driveway he could find and shut off the car. "Wait here."

"Like hell."

"Dot!"

"Chief!"

He sighed. "Fine. Stay behind me."

He got out of the car, drawing his gun. I walked swiftly around the back of the vehicle and did as he said. For once.

He slowed down and hid next to a large cedar bush in the neighbor's yard. He held his hand behind him, motioning me to wait. I peeked around him and saw the Connors' car, just sitting there, idling. Two minutes later, the car shut off, but nobody got out. My road was relatively unlit, rendering visibility into the vehicle to non-existent.

"What are they doing?" I whispered my question as close to Chief's ear as I could.

"I don't know. I can't see anything."

"The light just came on." I wanted to get closer to see better.

The door to the vehicle opened, and a blonde head emerged. Cindy, wearing a black jacket and dark pants, slipped out onto the street. She used her butt to slowly close the car door and walked around the back of the car, never taking her eyes off my house.

I wanted to sneak up behind her and scorch her where she stood. Chief held up a finger, never taking his eyes off her. When she started slinking toward my vehicle in my driveway, he slowly walked forward, waiting to see what she had planned.

Cindy stopped behind my vehicle, looking at the front of the house for any sign of movement. Satisfied that no one was watching, she skirted the vehicle and slipped up to the front door. Placing her palm over the deadbolt, I could hear her canting a spell, I just wasn't close enough to make out the words or read the intent.

I did, however, hear the front door unlock and watched as she slipped inside.

"Now," Chief whispered and he walked briskly up to the front of the house. Without waiting, he opened the front door and pointed his weapon and yelled, "Freeze!"

I could smell the smoke before I got to the door. "No. No. No. No."

I shoved Chief out of the way. The wall and door to my bedroom were on fire, smoke billowing up the vault in the ceiling. Cindy Connors stood there facing the door to the bedroom and shifted her glance back to me, surprised I wasn't in there. "What?"

I punched her in the face, knocking her to my newly renovated floors. "Bitch."

I looked at the merrily blazing fire burning through my walls. Panic started to fill me, and I couldn't think what to do. Chief pushed me to the side and held the arm not holding the gun out and yelled, "*Troi at garreg.*"

I watched as my board and plaster walls turned to stone, white paint becoming gray. Immediately the flames went out, its source of fuel transmuted to rock.

"Thanks, Chief."

"Nice punch."

Cindy Lou Whore groaned on my floor. I looked for a switch to beat the bitch.

I reached down and grabbed her with both my hands around the collar of her jacket, dragging her to the couch. Chief lent a hand before she woke up. "*Ceangail.*"

Ropes sprang from the couch beneath her, wrapping around her legs, chest, and arms. I willed them a little tighter, just to cause her a bit of discomfort when she woke up.

I leaned over and slapped her in the face a couple of times. She woke up after that. She glanced down at the bindings around her and sighed heavily. "You were supposed to be home."

"So, you did want to kill me."

She didn't say anything. I willed the bindings a little tighter, taking great satisfaction in seeing her pale face turn red. "Yes!"

The rope loosened a little. "Why?"

"Because."

"Because I'm dating Jimmy?"

"What?"

"Jimmy. Fireman? Really hot? You banged him. And Dennis. And a few other people you killed. Why?"

"Because you fucked my husband you whore!"

I shook my head. "Say that again slowly? Maybe it will make more sense this time?"

She blinked in confusion. "You slept with Blake."

"Um. No, I didn't?"

"Don't fucking lie. He told me."

"Chief?"

"Yeah."

"Can you just shoot her?" I was tired and angry. I sat down on the loveseat and rubbed the bridge of my nose, not wanting to deal with this bullshit.

"Not until we figure out what's going on," he answered and holstered his gun.

"Blake told you he slept with Dot?"

"Yes!"

"First of all, *if* she had, why would he tell you."

"Revenge. He wanted me to suffer."

"Why?"

"For cheating on him. I promised him I would stop. I did stop. But then he came home after the coven meeting and told me he fucked her in the closet of the firehouse."

"Okay, first. Ew. Your husband is a pig. I would rather sleep with a mule. Secondly, I didn't. That much I can fucking promise you."

Cindy looked utterly confused. "What?"

Apparently, Cindy wasn't playing with a full deck.

"Is that why you killed Dane and Richie, Cindy? Because you slept with them?"

"No? I didn't kill them. Except the woman. She had to die. She wanted my Blake. I couldn't let her take him. Burned her, I did."

I'd briefly spoken to Cindy at the firehouse and she'd seemed almost normal. She'd gone from zero to fruit bat in zero-point-three seconds. She stared at me and her eyes glazed, her irises going almost opaque. I snapped my fingers in front of her. She focused on my face, but just stared.

"You killed Rebecca?" Chief's voice sounded colder than the air outside. A shiver of fear ran up my spine.

"Yes. She wanted my Blake. He told me all the nasty things she wanted to do to him. He was afraid."

Chief drew his gun and I jumped in front of him. I didn't even blink as he screamed at me. I could see the gun shaking in his hand as his eyes went wide and all the rage he possessed threatened his sanity. He almost fired through me to get to her. I reached out and took the gun from his hand. "Easy, Chief. This is almost over."

I didn't blame him. I would have shot her, too. I still might.

Something still wasn't adding up. Especially the dim light in her eyes. I reached out, touching her head and immediately felt it. A spell clouding her judgement. "What the hell."

I felt like an idiot. I should have checked everyone for spells before. The only saving grace was her shield wasn't in place. That made things a little easier. "*Soiléir intinne.*"

It was like watching somebody remove cataracts. Her eyes went from milky to clear in an instant. She even shook her head and blinked. I expected her to be confused. Maybe even ask why she was there. She started sobbing uncontrollably instead.

"Cindy?" I repeated her name several more times. Finally, I cracked her across the cheek to get her to stop. She looked up at me, tears streaming down her face and the left side of her jaw swelling from my blow. "You there?"

She nodded. I ignored the look of hatred she gave me.

"Why did you kill the guys you slept with?"

"I didn't, you dumbass. Fucking Blake did it. He's probably after the other two right now. He used me as a distraction to get you away from the house. Hell, if he hadn't cast a beacon spell on the Chief's Jeep, he wouldn't have known you were there. He killed the other two." She turned and gave a little sigh of regret before turning her attention to

Chief. "He made me kill your wife, and now he wants me to do the same thing to your new piece of ass."

She snarled and struggled against her bonds.

"Chief…"

"Leave her for now. Text Josie and have her come home and hold a knife to her throat. If what she says is true…"

"I know. We'll deal with it after." What?

"One way or another."

Chapter 27

I was out of the car before Chief put it into park. I ran for the front door ready to blast Blake into the ninth pit of hell. The front door had already been kicked open and my heart sank that we were too late.

I trudged through the trashed house, not even bothering to step over the smashed glasses, mugs, and pictures. I headed straight for where I knew I'd find their bodies. Jimmy, lying dead in his bed, was already etched into my mind. I closed my eyes and turned the corner. His mattress was flipped and his room destroyed, but he wasn't there.

I dashed to Dennis' room and found the same thing.

"What the fuck is going on?"

Chief was standing there holding his gun pointed at the ceiling. My phone rang.

It was Jimmy.

I'd called him thirteen times on the way over and he never answered.

"Where the fuck are you?"

"Hello to you, too?"

"Now is not the time, Jimmy. Where...are...you."

"Just leaving the bar. Sorry I didn't hear my phone."

I dropped to my knees in the middle of his living room and started hyperventilating. They were still alive. "You're an asshole. I thought I lost you." The tears started streaming down my cheeks.

"What's going on?"

"Leave the bar. Blake is on the loose and he's trying to kill you. Chief and I are at your house. Meet me at mine. If you see Blake, run or scorch him from the earth."

"Roger. On our way."

"So, if Cindy had the car, how did Blake get here? It's not like Jimmy's house is within walking distance. They live on the other side of town." Chief's voice still had an edge to it. He was out for blood.

"I don't know. They only have one vehicle?"

"This is Cedar Falls, Dot. Most people only have one vehicle."

"Maybe he stole one? I don't know."

"That's going to make finding him a little difficult."

"We won't have to. He came here and Jimmy and Dennis weren't. He's heading to my house to see if we are there and finish off Cindy if she failed!"

We raced to the car and got back in it. I was tired of being a day late and a dollar short. Chief gunned it and flipped on the siren. I white knuckled the dash all the way back to the house, only letting go to text Josie. She assured me they were fine. She and Candace were watching Cindy and the windows. My phone rang as we screeched to a stop in the front of the house.

"We're here, Josie."

"I know. I saw the blue lights and figured it was time to end playtime. See, that's the thing about texts, *Lady*. You're never quite sure who is on the other end..."

"Blake?"

"Yes."

"Where is Josie?"

"Alive for now. I see you caught my failure of a wife."

"Yeah. She wasn't exactly all there."

"She's had years of spells layered upon her mind. I'm surprised she doesn't drool on herself."

"Why?" I flipped my phone on speaker so Chief could hear.

"Why what?"

"Everything. Why are you doing all this?"

"Well, she deserved it."

"Who?"

"My cheating whore of a wife. She killed Becca. She slept with every man she could dig her hooks into. I wanted to make her life a living hell before I wiped her off the face of the earth."

"Have you?"

"Oh, yes. Quite well. I don't think I could have tormented her any more. I wanted to kill her last two lovers, but I don't even think she had enough sanity left to truly appreciate what I've done. Such a pity. That just means she has nothing else to live for."

Bang!

"Blake! What did you do?"

"Put her out of my misery. That chapter is over. Now it's time for me to go. I need you and the Chief to back away from the Cherokee. I'll be taking that to make my getaway."

"Like hell you will," Chief growled angrily.

Another gunshot and a scream echoed from the inside of the house. The screaming continued long after the shot was fired.

"I killed the little blonde. I still have your best friend. She will be accompanying me to the edge of town. In the Chief's car. If we don't see anyone following us, I'll let her go. You may pick her up after I'm gone. I'll let her have her phone back."

"How can we trust you?"

"You can't. But you don't have a choice. I can shoot her now, if you prefer?"

"No! Come out. We're backing away from the vehicle now."

I got out and waited for Chief to do the same. He did, albeit reluctantly. "This is a bad idea. He's going to kill her anyway."

"No, he's not," I answered firmly.

"How do you know?"

"Because I'm going to kill him."

"What are you going to do, Dot? Dot?"

I ignored him.

"Throw the gun up by the door, Chief."

Chief sighed and lightly tossed it into the tuft of juniper by the walkway. "There."

"Now go stand over there," he pointed with the gun to the neighbor's driveway.

We started backing up. The further we got, the more he came out the front door. He had one arm around Josie, the gun pointed at the side of her head. When they made it halfway, I started walking toward him. He paused and made a threatening gesture with the arm holding the gun. I held up my hands.

"I'm not trying anything stupid. I want you to take me. Leave Josie. I'll go with you. Same plan, different hostage."

"Fine. I'd rather have you, anyway."

"Dot, *no*!"

"Not your choice, Chief," I called back sadly.

"Come stand in front of me and turn around."

I did exactly as he said, blocking Chief's view. Keeping my arms up, I felt the barrel of the gun press against the base of my skull.

Blake pushed Josie to the ground. She didn't move, other than to cover her head with her arms. Blake's arm wrapped around my waist and he backed us up to the open-doored Jeep waiting for his escape. He pushed me down into my seat, never taking the gun off me as he walked around the front of the vehicle. I didn't move.

I almost breathed a sigh of relief when he got into the car and started the engine. He put it in gear and gunned the engine, slamming the doors shut with the inertia.

He kept the gun pointed at me all the way to the end of my street. There was one thing I'd noticed about Chief's vehicle. The power steering on it was a stone-cold bitch. Chief's muscular forearms probably wouldn't be half as impressive if he didn't spend so much time in his beloved Jeep. It almost made me sad for what I was about to do.

Halfway through the turn, when he absolutely needed both hands to avoid hitting the large oak a little *too* close to the curb, I whispered, "*Craiceann cosúil le cloch.*"

He felt the power of the spell before he heard my canting. Blake let go of the wheel, not caring if we hit the tree or not and swung the gun in my direction, pulling the trigger.

"*Seomra dócháin,*" I called out in a grating voice.

The bullet left the barrel of the gun in a tuft of fire, spinning as it sailed directly at my chest as time slowed to a crawl. The corner of my mouth lifted in a wicked grin as the bullet struck me and shattered. Most of it went outward, shattering the windshield as the interior of the Cherokee became an inferno. My first spell had turned my skin into stone, much like Chief had done to my walls. It would only last for a moment before shattering with my need to breathe. My second spell turned Chief's Jeep into a combustion chamber, the fire of the gun being the only catalyst needed. The temperatures reached a thousand degrees instantaneously, sucking all the air out of it before extinguishing itself.

A second later, we crashed headlong into the Oak tree he'd been so desperate to avoid. The air bags went off. My increased mass shattered mine like a water balloon. Blake hit his and cracked like a husk, all the moisture having been flashed from his body.

The wheels of the Jeep went round and round, burning the tires down on the rims as we had nowhere to go. When my spell finally wore off, I reached over and shut the engine off before I fell out the door, landing on the pavement below. I puked the entire contents of my stomach and lungs onto the street. Looking up, I saw several figures running toward me. The image burned itself into my brain as I passed out.

Chapter 28

I woke up, staring at my familiar ceiling. I was lying in the middle of my bed, Chief on one side of me and Jimmy snoring soundly on the other. Both were holding some part of my body. It was a nice way to wake up.

"How you feeling?"

"I've been better, Chief. What happened?"

"Your little stunt almost cost you your life. Your spell protected you from the blast of fire, but it only protected your skin. Some of the flames found their way into your lungs. You might want to cover your face with your hands next time."

"There isn't going to be a next time. That was my Hail Mary pass. Once in a lifetime play. Gonna rip that page out of the old playbook." I hated sports. I just hoped I didn't sound like an idiot to Chief.

"I like that plan even better. By the way, you're still kind of hot bald."

"Wha?" I reached up and felt the top of my head. The skin tingled under the palm of my hand. "Fuck."

"Relax, you can magic it back."

"I know, but still. You've been having to stare at my bald ass all night."

"Yep. Your ass is bald. There isn't a single hair left on your body."

"And how do you know all this? Did you actually check, perv?'

"Didn't have to. You canted a stone skin spell on yourself. Next time you might want to combine that with a stone hair and clothes spell."

"Shit. I should have just gone with the stone shield again. That worked better."

"No. Stone shit might hurt coming out. I was constipated once. Nasty business."

Chief made me smile. I leaned over and gently gave him a kiss.

"Can I get one of those?"

I looked behind me at Jimmy, smiling at our exchange. I leaned over and gave him one, too. Very happy to see him very much alive. I sighed and leaned back on my pillow.

"So. How bad is everything else?"

"Town is calling you a hero. You crashed the kidnapper's escape vehicle into a tree, just as it caught fire and narrowly getting out yourself. He wasn't kidding, though. He put a bullet through Cindy's head."

I gulped, fearing the answer to my next question. "Candace?"

"Should be up in a few days. He shot her in the chest, thinking that would simply be the end of her. As soon you left in the Jeep, she came stumbling out of the house, wheezing, but very much alive. Apparently, because of her fae blood, she doesn't take a whole lot of damage from metals that aren't iron. I keep mine loaded with silver. It kills bad guys and the occasional werewolf. I learned that lesson the hard way."

"You've actually had a werewolf terrorize the town?"

"He was a transient. Nice enough guy until the full moon."

"We have a family in Ashville. They spend full moons in the local jail."

"I'll keep that in mind next time one comes into town."

"What about Josie. She okay?"

"She's fine. Taking care of Candace. Happily, I might add."

I nodded. Satisfied. "Dennis okay?"

"Yeah. He went home to start cleaning up the house. Chief told us what happened," Jimmy said angrily.

"Well, I need a shower. I smell like a barbeque."

"Need some help?"

They both asked at the exact same moment...

I said, "Okay," and crawled over Chief. I shucked the tank top and shorts *someone* had slipped on me and waltzed my bald ass into the bathroom.

I looked over my shoulder to find Chief and Jimmy staring at each other across the bed.

"You guys coming?"

Epilogue

I smiled at the witches gathered at my table. Even though the killers had been caught, I figured a little celebration was in order. I sat myself at the head of the table and lifted my glass of wine.

"A toast to the Coven of the First Moon. We were tested even as we began, and we survived. We are fewer in number and lost friends along the way. May our future be brighter and safer."

They all lifted their glasses, expressions sad and hopeful.

"My bookstore will be done in a few months. This is the first step on a long road to recovery. Josie and I come from a small town where witches and humans live together in harmony. It is a prosperous town filled with fun and happiness. Most of our strife was centered around my mother and her love of tormenting opponents, human *and* witch, with carefully planned spells left to humiliate. That is what I want for this town, minus the pranking. I want to see Cedar Falls as it should be. I'm going to need the coven's help with this. Are you all in agreement?"

"Aye," was shouted from the nine of them in front of me.

"Good. Let's dig in. It's Italian night!"

They stood and chatted as they got in line, serving themselves from the giant foil pans Herb had delivered. The food smelled delicious.

"Not bad for the first week in town, huh?" Josie laughed.

I looked over at her and gave her a crooked grin.

"Oh, sweetie. Don't smile like that without the hair. You look like a deranged bowling ball. When are you going to grow it back?"

"Probably tonight. I kind of liked the feeling until I went outside. Screw that. I think my brain froze a little."

She started chuckling, rubbing Candace's shoulder as the smaller woman wrapped her arms around her from the side. The sight of the two of them together warmed my heart. Candace had become a part of the family in every way.

"What are we talking about?" Jimmy slipped up behind me, wrapping his arms around me and giving my neck a kiss.

"Growing my hair back."

"Soon?"

"Tonight."

"Sweet."

"You don't like my bowling ball?"

"Well, it's not that I don't dislike it…"

His double negative wasn't lost on me. I swatted his arm and faked a good pout. He kissed the top of my head and then polished it with his sleeve.

"Just kidding. You'd be beautiful with a purple mohawk. I'm just partial to sexy redheads."

He left to get in line and fill his plate.

"Purple mohawk?" Josie asked with an evil grin.

"Bet your ass," I replied, nodding.

Candace giggled conspiratorially.

Chief ran his hand over my back and gave my butt a little squeeze as he sneaked past me, getting in line behind Jimmy. His intimate gesture didn't go unnoticed by Josie. She cocked an eyebrow at me and shook her head.

"How the hell do you have two boyfriends that are totally okay with it?"

I shrugged. "Just fucking lucky, I guess. That and I'm a queen bee or something."

Candace let go of Josie and wrapped her arms around me, pressing her face against my chest. I was getting used to it. She craved the affection. I stroked her hair and continued my conversation with Josie until the doorbell caught everyone's attention.

"That's weird. I'll get it. Everybody keep eating."

I dislodged Candace and walked through the living room. I looked through the peephole. A man I'd never seen before stood on my stoop, blinking at the bright overhead light.

Curious, I opened the door.

"Dorothea Blackwell?"

"Yes?"

"Forgive my intrusion, may I speak to you?"

"Yes. Won't you come in?"

"Are you giving me permission?"

"If you're not here to hurt me, then yes. Please come in."

He sighed gratefully and stepped inside. "I am sorry. I had hoped to speak to you alone, but time is not on my side. It wasn't my intention to disrupt your party."

"That's okay. What can I do for you?"

"My clan is in trouble. I would ask for the help of the Coven of the First Moon," he said formally and put his hand over his chest, bowing low.

"Your clan?"

"Yes," he answered respectfully and smiled.

His fangs became quite visible in the warm light of my living room.

He was a vampire.

And I'd just invited him in…

Available now!

About the Author

A late comer to the writing game, Jacquelyn had always been a fan of romance novels and lately become addicted to the reverse harem category. I mean seriously, who wouldn't? Sitting alone one night she flipped open her laptop and said, "I'm going to give this a whirl." And thus, the Lovin' the Coven series was given life. She has designs on other series as well, but only time shall tell.

As for her, she is five-foot-something, with graying hair, wicked eyes, an eager smile, and an annoying laugh. She lives at home with her dog, a cat, and that is about all she is comfortable sharing.

Other Works

Lovin' the Coven Series

First Moon
Second Blood
Third Charm (Coming Soon!)